ADAM'S REDEMPTION

RAWLINS Book 4

DEBORAH WALLACE

Adam's Redemption: Rawlins Book 4

Published by Deborah Wallace

10/22

ISBN 978-1-951457-04-4

Cover Art by Raymond and Deborah Wallace
Rawlins town by Raymond Wallace

Chapter 1

Adam Richards slumped in the chair, Dr. Andrews across the desk from him. After spending two hours a week for five months in this cozy office—soft instrumental music in the background, room lit by wall sconces, and a ceiling painted to represent a warm, blue sky and fluffy summer clouds—he'd had his fill of heart wrenching conversations disguised in tranquility.

The doctor cleared her throat. "I'm proud of you. I know burning those pictures was one of the hardest things you had to do, but it's proof to yourself that you're over the obsession. You've come a long way."

He blew out a breath, and stared at his laced hands. He rarely looked her in the eye in these sessions. "It was hard, but it felt good, too. I felt…lighter with each stack of prints I threw into the flames." He glanced to her face and down again. He wouldn't tell her that he'd cried. And it wasn't stacks. He viewed each picture of Jamie one last time before tossing it into the fireplace. It needed to be done to break the last tie with her—fifteen years of pictures, watching her grow up.

Dr. Andrews had delivered him from the brink of madness. He'd spent a month trapped in a psych ward at the hospital, half of which he couldn't remember. Two weeks of anti-psychotic drugs and sessions with Dr. Andrews had brought him to his senses enough to not talk about abilities. Almost anyone would consider a person delusional if he rambled on about someone creating lightning strikes, or causing pain with a glare.

The doctor tapped the pen on her notebook, a sign the session was almost over. Adam rubbed his hands over the tops of his thighs, then ran a hand through his fairly short, dark hair.

She dropped her notebook onto her lap. "You've fulfilled your six months of psychological visits Judge Winslow suggested, but I think you'd benefit from continuing our sessions. There are still some issues with your family you should deal with."

He didn't want to see her anymore. They'd hashed through his relationships with his father and Art enough already. Further discussions wouldn't improve his opinions of them. He got the feeling Dr. Andrews wanted to tarnish the memories of his mother. He'd had to shut her down on a few occasions when her questions suggested his mother hadn't always acted in his best interest. His mom had been blind to anything that made his father appear evil, and that's the way his father wanted it. That knowledge might have changed his sweet mother, and he'd needed her exactly the way she'd been.

"Dr. Andrews, I feel really good about myself now. Thanks to you, my obsession with Jamie is gone. I know now how it was fostered by my father. I'll do better not thinking about them."

The doctor had advised against him visiting his father in prison while he was under her care, feeling he needed to understand his relationship with his father first. He had no inclination to ever see his dad again, so it didn't matter.

Adam rose and wiped his hands down his pant legs. "I know I'd still be in that hospital without you, and I really appreciate all you've done for me, but I'm ready to stand on my own two feet again."

The doctor set aside her note pad and stood, coming to the shoulder of his six-two frame. "I wish you'd reconsider. Remember, you can come back if you need to."

"I'll keep that in mind." Maybe he should hug her, but her stiff posture held him back. She probably had her mind on her next patient. "Anyway, thanks for everything."

She held her hand out, palm down, and he took it in both his. Maybe she'd noticed his hesitation. Sometimes she seemed to be a mind reader. "You're welcome. Take care of yourself."

Adam released her and left the office. Down the hall, past the elevator, he hit the handle on the door to the stairs and raced down the six flights, so full of energy, he couldn't stand still to take the elevator. He hit the lobby and slowed to a fast jaunt out to the sidewalk, then leaped into the air and punched his fist skyward. "Yes!"

One passerby chuckled and another shook his head.

Adam didn't care. He was free. Free to do what, he didn't know. The inheritance from his maternal grandmother had sustained him the past six months, and would for his entire life, but he'd become bored. He could search for an investment job to replace the one he'd lost.

Adam rounded a pile of dirty snow, got in his car and drove through teeth grinding Boston traffic to the Beacon Hill area. He turned through the opening in the wrought iron fence into the single space beside his townhouse—one of the few residences with off-street parking—depressed the button opening his garage door and closed it behind him. His home was the last in a long line of attached red brick houses with white trim. He barreled through the house door, coming into the kitchen.

Home sweet home. His grandparents had lived here, and

he'd enjoyed visiting them, especially the times his parents left Art and him for a week or so while they traveled. The house was three blocks from Boston Common, so he and his brother had spent a lot of time chasing each other through the park. Art liked to chase the squirrels and torment the swans, so Adam used to distract his brother, getting Art to chase him instead.

The home had become his three years ago when his grandmother died. He'd been closer to her than his father, and he still missed her.

Art had inherited his grandparents' country house in Shelburne Falls. It was larger than this one and they'd spent several weeks every summer there. He'd been disappointed when Art had sold it almost immediately.

Adam tossed his keys into the chunky blue bowl on the small table beside the door. Maybe he should leave for a couple of weeks, take time to figure out what he wanted to do. He'd finished reevaluating his investments and they could take care of themselves for a while.

He sighed and headed for the living room. Adam paused when his head spun, a sure sign that a premonition had overtaken him. He grabbed his head and sank to his knees on the hardwood floor.

***

A woman lay on a dining room table, eyes closed, and features slack. The overhead light glistened on her thick, dark hair and golden skin. High cheekbones spoke of her Native American heritage. Her chest rose and fell in an even rhythm. Black pants were dragged down to her knees and a red flowered shirt bunched at the top of her pregnant belly.

Adam sucked in his breath as Art stepped into view carrying a hunting knife. He set it down, and opened a book, the oldest spell book in their father's library. Every spell was geared to do some kind of evil—cause pain, compel compliance, or increase powers by various means. Art gazed at the page.

His lips formed into a cruel smile, the one he used when they were kids and he was about to hurt a neighbor's pet or tease one of the less attractive girls at school. Art lit three black candles and set the candelabra at the woman's shoulder. He fished a piece of chalk from his pocket and glanced again at the book and drew on the table. He referred to the page again and again, scrawling more diagrams on either side of the woman, then stuffed the chalk back into his pocket.

Art picked up the knife and sliced into the woman's belly near the pubic area. She didn't flinch, and Adam wondered if she'd been drugged or put under a spell.

Adam cringed and lunged for his brother, passing through him. From the many premonitions he'd witnessed, Adam knew he was a helpless observer, but his reaction was instinctive.

Art ran a finger along the cut and sliced some more. He set down the knife and reached into the rift and tugged. First a tiny baby leg appeared, then the other, followed by the whole body. A tiny, premature boy. Blood and water gushed from the ragged perforation.

The little body dangled upside down, arms waving and a weak cry came from the crinkled face.

Art jerked and swore as he nearly dropped the baby on his mother's belly. His brother wrapped a small towel around the child, and lifted him again. The cloth wasn't to keep the baby warm, but to give Art a better grip.

Art stared at the book, and held the baby to the full extent that the umbilical cord allowed. He glanced back at the page, then set the squirming child back on his mother. With the knife, he cut the umbilical cord.

Art lifted the baby higher this time, and began reading aloud. "Blood of my blood, life of my life, I offer my child up as a conduit of your power. I beg you to pass your power through this innocent so that I may serve you more fully."

This baby was Art's own son.

Electricity crackled and a streak of purple lightning struck the baby, feeding energy into him for at least a minute. Art closed his eyes and smiled.

The energy dissipated and Art laid the child, face down, across his mother's distended belly. His cry was weaker than the first one. The poor child was dying.

Art used the towel to wipe down the candelabra and the knife handle, then with a swift lunge, thrust the blade into the woman's chest. He picked up the book, and strode away. A door closed nearby.

"No!" Adam had never witnessed anything so abhorrent.

Chapter 2

Adam opened his pale blue eyes, and wiped his wet cheeks. He lay on his side on the floor of the short hallway that led to the living room.

He needed to find that woman and save her. If the woman and child were his, he'd do everything in his power to protect them from someone like Art. Someone who shouldn't be allowed to gain that kind of power, whatever it was. He had no idea how much time he had to rescue the woman, since his premonition might happen in a day, a week or months.

He scrambled up from the floor, recalling one morning while captive, Jamie had been taken to the gym, and his brother had come in to taunt him, asking if Jamie was good in bed. Adam wouldn't answer him and his brother had rightly assumed they hadn't had sex. Art had gloated, said their father wouldn't care which of them got Jamie pregnant. He'd enjoy taking her into one of the other basement rooms and giving her what Adam wouldn't. Fortunately, she'd been rescued before Art got the chance.

Maybe his father had only wanted a child of his blood so he could perform the transfer of power spell Adam had seen in the vision. It could have been the real reason his father had kidnapped Jamie. Now, with their father in prison, Art wanted to be the one to use the spell. Adam wouldn't let him.

That woman and her baby needed to be rescued, and Adam was the only one who could do it.

***

Adam stopped at the curb in front of Art's house, a large gambrel in a nice neighborhood. It exude a wave of revulsion. Probably a spell to keep people away. Art bought the home after selling the one he'd inherited. Adam had visited shortly after the purchase, but had been told he wasn't welcome.

An unfamiliar black BMW sat inside the open garage. Adam had stopped by the day before and earlier in the day, but no one answered his knock.

Art was a live-in-the-moment type of guy, and hopefully, wouldn't speculate on Adam's visit. Art wasn't stupid, he just never thought situations or his actions through.

Adam was a planner, but too often, his father had trampled his plans. One that he'd encouraged was Jamie. Adam mapped out a life with her, and that had ended when she'd been carried off by the man she loved.

Now his brother appeared to have an obsession—to gain power through an unborn baby.

Adam blew out a breath. He had to get his head in the game and deal with Art. Any distractions could get him hurt.

He marched up to the door and rang the bell. He snickered. Beethoven's Fifth. That was so not Art. It must have been already programmed when he bought the house.

The door was yanked open and Art glared. They both had dark brown hair with a hint of curl. Art wore his a bit longer. Where Adam's eyes were a clear blue like their mother, Art's were the deepest brown. Art towered over Adam, his bulk and height. "What are you doing here?"

"Nice to see you, too, little brother. Now that I'm free of

that psychologist, I figured we could catch up."

Art filled the doorway and folded his arms across his chest. "I think they should have kept you. I don't want to know about your life, and there's no way I'm telling you about mine."

Adam squeezed past Art's arms. "How's Dad? I haven't been allowed to visit him." Even if he was his father's favorite son, there was no way in hell Adam was going to see him. Thanks to his therapy sessions, Adam finally understood how screwed up their relationship was.

Adam followed the maple floor from the small foyer into the living room and sat on a tan leather sofa. A huge flat screen TV hung over a ceramic tiled fireplace. Three pieces of splashy modern art graced the other cream colored walls. It would be a comfortable room if it wasn't occupied by his brother.

Art stalked behind him and huffed before dropping onto a matching recliner. "Why do you care? It's your fault he's in prison."

Adam stiffened. As if. "My fault? Dad kidnapped me—with your help. Was it my fault Jamie's family wouldn't stop searching for her? Was it my fault Dad told the police the truth about kidnapping me, too?"

Art sprang up and towered over Adam, his hands fisted at his sides. "And if you'd knocked Jamie up sometime during your four years at college with her, Dad wouldn't have had to resort to something so drastic."

Adam shoved up from the couch, their faces inches apart. "I was supposed to marry her, not disrespect her."

Art snorted. "You think Dad cared how you made a baby with her?"

Adam dropped back to the sofa. They'd been betrothed at Jamie's birth when he was five. If her birth parents hadn't died, they probably would have grown up together, but instead, he'd been fed a steady diet of Jamie through pictures that he'd come to realize had been taken unknowingly.

All those years, he'd thought the purpose was to join two powerful families. "But he wanted me to love her." He'd come face-to-face with Jamie her first day of college, and fell in love. At least he thought he had, but it was the crazy obsession. He cared about her, and was happy she'd found a guy who truly loved her. Now, relief was all he felt that this particular plan of his father had failed.

"Ha! Because he knew you wouldn't marry her otherwise. You're too soft. I don't know why you were his favorite." Art fisted his hand and poked his chest with his thumb. "But now I'm his favorite. I don't need love to make a baby. I don't even have to like her."

He'd never realized his father only cared about getting a grandchild. His father had always seemed sincere when he talked about Jamie and Adam marrying.

Art sneered. "A couple years ago, I tried to talk Dad into letting me go after Jamie, but he wouldn't hear of it."

Adam shivered. He couldn't imagine—and didn't want to—what Art would have done to get Jamie pregnant. He sent up silent thanks that his father hadn't given in, no matter the reason.

Art raised his voice. "He would have had power by now, if not for your incompetence."

Adam frowned. They were getting to his purpose in coming. "What's power got to do with grandchildren?"

"Do you really think he cares about grandchildren?"

Adam raised his eyebrows. "Yeah. Carry on the legacy and all that."

Art shook his head. "Maybe eventually. But he wanted more power now. So I'm going to get it instead. And break him out of that hole he's in."

"How are you going to do that?" Hopefully, Art wanted

to brag more than keep his secret.

Art smirked. "I scried for a powerful woman. Good for me she was so naive. She's pretty, too." He waved his hand at his chest. "Between my sparkling personality and a love spell, I got what I wanted."

Adam scanned the room. There were no womanly touches. "Where is she?"

Art raised his brows. "I don't keep her here. She's too big to be fun anymore, but I check up on her."

A slight relief relaxed Adam's shoulders. The woman was still alive. He might still have time to save her, but if Art thought she was too big, her death was more likely days away.

Adam stood and shook his head. "I don't know you anymore. I'm out of here." He headed for the door.

"You never knew me."

Adam wrapped his hand around the doorknob, but Art held the door closed. Adam faced him.

Art squinted. "I don't know why you came here, but don't come back. Next time you might not be able to leave."

Adam straightened to his full height. "Fine. I don't want a brother like you anyway." He yanked the door open and stalked outside. The door slammed behind him.

He'd drive up the street and wait for Art to leave and follow him. Maybe they'd end up at the woman's place.

The open garage door caught his eye. The BMW. He could hide something in it and use a find spell later to track it. He shoved his hands in his pockets and pulled out the contents. He could use a credit card, but if Art found it, he'd know immediately what Adam was doing, and destroy it. His pen. It was a half-length pen he'd gotten as a graduation present. No initials, and Art probably wouldn't recognize it.

Now, where to hide it? The trunk. He held his hand over the lock, and concentrated on the mechanism. After a few moments, there was a soft click and the lid popped up an inch. He lifted it and stared inside. The new car smell hit him, as well as its emptiness. There was nothing to hide the pen under. Maybe under the mat. He could drop the pen in with the spare tire, but there was the slim chance that Art would have a flat tire and find it. The rubber seal. He shoved the pen behind the rubber seal halfway between the hinges. It couldn't be seen. He nudged the trunk lid closed. It hadn't bound against the pen. Perfect.

His father had known about his unlocking skill, which was why there'd always been a guard posted outside the door when he was held captive.

Adam hurried to his car and drove away, taking the first right, then left, to parallel his brother's street, and stopped at the curb beside an empty lot. Hidden, but not far away.

From the glove box, he fished out an eagle talisman, held it in his fist and closed his eyes, imagining the pen he'd left behind. "What I have lost, I must now find. Lead me to this object of mine."

He looped the chain over his rear view mirror and steadied the swing. The eagle turned until the beak pointed back and to Adam's left. The car was still in Art's garage. He stared at the talisman, sat back and waited.

Chapter 3

Adam's gaze never left the talisman. Nearly two hours and it hadn't twisted. He shifted in his seat for the fourth time and tipped his head from side to side. His muscles had started to cramp. Maybe he should give up and try again tomorrow.

A tap on his window startled him. A policeman. Wonderful. He hoped he didn't get arrested. What would his psychologist say, the day after his last appointment?

He twisted the key to accessory and rolled down the window. "Hi, officer."

The man's gaze darted around the interior and back to Adam's face. "I got a call that you've been sitting in your car here for a while. Mind telling me why?"

I put a tracker on my brother's car and I'm waiting for him to drive somewhere. No. That wouldn't do. He rubbed his hand down his face. "I had some things to think through away from everything familiar. This seemed as good a place as any." A lot had gone through his mind while he sat here, so it wasn't a total lie.

"May I see ID?"

"I'm not doing anything wrong."

The officer narrowed his eyes and held his hand out. "Just pass it over."

Adam extracted his wallet from his back pocket, flipped it open and handed the officer his license.

The other man flicked it. "I'll be right back."

Adam drummed his thumbs on the steering wheel as three long minutes passed before the officer returned and handed Adam his license. The man rested his hand on the butt of his gun. Adam swallowed and wished he could take a swig from his bottle of water.

"You haven't actually done anything wrong, but I'd suggest you find somewhere else to park."

Adam hoped there would be no burglaries in the neighborhood in the near future because he'd be the first person the police would suspect. "Sure, officer. Maybe I'll go find a…parking lot."

The man glared. "You do that." He tapped the side of Adam's car and stalked back to his own.

Adam returned his license to his wallet and pocket, started the car and glanced at the eagle. It had changed direction.

Art was on the move.

Adam wished it had happened ten minutes sooner. After a glance in the rear view mirror, he shifted the car to drive and rolled down the street.

Art seemed to parallel this street, so Adam continued straight. The talisman swung a bit from driving, but maintained a steady direction.

Adam stopped at an intersection and the eagle gradually turned. Art sped past on the road crossing his.

Adam let a few cars get between them and took a right to follow. Art turned into a grocery store parking lot and Adam continued past. He took the next corner and entered the lot at the side, backing into a space in employee parking.

Likely, Art would get his food and go home, but Adam would track him anyway, just in case. Thirty minutes later, Art left the store carrying four plastic bags. He passed several cars before stopping at his own, and placed the bags in the trunk.

Art backed out of his space and headed towards the side exit. He wasn't headed home.

Adam ducked down, and waited a minute before following. He drove slow enough so as not to catch up with Art. Three times, he slowed as the eagle twisted, and almost missed the turns. Fifteen minutes from the store, the talisman pointed left at a driveway. Trees only allowed a partial view of the tan colored house that sat back from the road.

He made a u-turn a few houses up and slowed as he passed again, marking the location on his phone GPS. Since Art took groceries to the woman, Adam assumed the sacrifice wouldn't be for at least a few days. He'd come back tomorrow.

***

Adam left his house at seven-thirty, hoping to catch the woman at home, if she worked. He still didn't have an excuse to get inside.

Flowers. Every girl loved getting flowers. He stopped at a grocery store and picked up a bouquet of daisies arranged in a yellow metal watering can. He hoped that would get him in the door.

A half-hour later, he drove down her street. As he turned into the driveway, he noticed four mailboxes beside it. Apartments. Of course, it wouldn't be easy.

The driveway lead to the back of the building, where four parking spaces spanned it, and another four lined the edge of the lush lawn. A varnished picnic table sat on the grass. Three cars were parked near the building and one more at the grass. He parked beside the lone car. Two doors overlooked a twelve-by-twelve deck. Two more, on the second floor, required climbing a set of stairs beside the deck.

He didn't have a name to use, and couldn't knock on a door and tell the responder he was searching for a pregnant woman. They'd tell him to leave or they'd call the police.

A man exited the left-most door, got into a Jeep SUV, and drove away. Most likely, she wasn't in his apartment.

Adam picked up the flowers and took determined steps to the second door on the deck. He knocked, and the wrong woman opened the door.

Her gaze dropped to the flowers and back to his face.

He should have thought this through. "Hi. I heard my pregnant friend wasn't feeling well, and I thought I'd cheer her up. Obviously, I got the address wrong."

Her eyes lit up. "Oh, you mean Trill?" She pointed up. "She lives above me. I've noticed she hasn't been herself."

"Thanks." He lifted the watering can. "I hope this cheers her up." That was easier than he expected.

He ascended the stairs and dragged in a breath. Trill's life depended on him being able to convince her she was in danger from a man she obviously trusted. He stiffened his shoulders and knocked on the door. After a minute, he knocked again.

Art couldn't have done the sacrifice last night. He'd given her groceries. A chill zipped down his spine. Maybe he'd bought them for himself, intending on taking them home after he stopped here. If Adam had thought of that last night, he would have gone in and interrupted. He hoped he wasn't too late.

The door opened and the woman from his vision stood before him. She stood about six inches shorter than his six-foot-two, and was five or six months pregnant. Her unfocused gaze rested on his face. She was beautiful. Her sun-kissed skin complemented golden brown eyes. The perfect straight nose led to full lips.

He sucked in a breath, and reminded himself he had to

save this woman. "Hi. I'm Adam Richards, Art's brother. I need to talk to you."

She tipped her head. "I don't think Art has a brother."

"Yeah, I don't tell people about him either. It's really important that I talk to you."

She stepped back. "I probably shouldn't let you in." Her voice held no inflection.

He handed her the bouquet. "I brought you these."

Her expression didn't change. "No one's ever given me flowers before. I love daisies. I used to pick them for my mother." She tipped her head, as if considering him. "Come on in."

He followed her inside. She set them in the center of her dining room table, the one he'd seen in his vision. The one she'd die on if he couldn't convince her to leave.

She touched her necklace, a moonstone surrounded by an intricate silver braid.

He squinted at it. There was something…"May I?"

Her hand enclosed the stone, then she released it and nodded.

He took the pendant between his fingers. Soothing vibes emanated from it. Too soothing. Maybe that's why she seemed a bit dazed. Another feeling pulsed from it. Longing for Art.

He clenched his fist around the pendant, anger for Art enhancing his power. He thrust energy into the stone, warming it. He opened his hand. The white stone had turned a lifeless gray and had cracked. With a hand gripped on the chain at each side of the pendant, he yanked it apart and let the pieces drop to the floor.

Trill's eyes widened, then closed and she crumpled. He scooped her up before she hit the floor, marched into the living room, and laid her on the couch. He crouched in front of her, and ran his fingertips over her soft cheek. "Trill.

You're okay now. Trill."

Even unconscious, she was beautiful. How could his brother plan on killing this woman? He was heartless.

Adam had barely met the woman and his feelings of protectiveness had multiplied.

Her eyes fluttered open, and she strained away from him.

"Easy. I'm here to help you."

She drew in a deep breath, sat up, and rubbed her forehead. Her eyes widened and she placed a hand on each side of her belly. "Oh. My. God. I'm pregnant. I feel like I just woke from a long dream." She stared down at her belly. "Or a nightmare." Trill raked her hands through her hair. "The last I remember, I wasn't pregnant. How did I get pregnant? Did you do this?"

He took her hand and rubbed his thumb over it. "No. Not me. I'm sorry. I want to help you."

Her hand trembled, but she didn't snatch it away. "Help with what? Who did you say you were?"

"Adam Richards. Art's brother."

Her forehead crinkled. "Art? I went out with him once. I didn't like his energy and refused to go out with him again." She bit her lip and her gaze darted to his. She probably regretted mentioning energy.

Anger boiled up, but Adam tamped it down. "He put a spelled necklace on you to make you compliant. I just broke it."

Her hands rubbed over her belly. He couldn't tell if it was to sooth herself or the baby or to convince herself it was true. Her eyes widened and she sucked in a breath. "The baby just moved. I can't believe I'm pregnant."

He nodded. "Art impregnated you." He couldn't say it was Art's baby. No way would he allow Art to get anywhere near this woman and her child.

"I don't understand." She'd mentioned Art's energy, so

maybe she understood a little.

Adam wanted to gather her into his arms, but he was a stranger and the brother of the man who'd wronged her. And he wouldn't blame her. "Art searched for a woman with power and found you. He wants more power and made this baby with you, so it could be a conduit for him to increase his power."

Her hands drew circles on her stomach, and her gaze remained on the unexpected life she harbored. It had to be a huge shock to wake from a dream world and find out she was this far along in a pregnancy. She glanced at him. "So he doesn't have to sacrifice the baby for this power ceremony?"

"He doesn't, but he will." It still angered him that his brother planned to kill this woman and baby when it wasn't necessary. Not that he'd approve killing for any reason, other than self-defense.

"How do you know that?"

He took her hand. "Because I saw it in a premonition."

She bit her lip. "Can I see?"

Even if he could, he wouldn't show her how she and the baby would die. "I'm not able to do that."

"I can. May I touch you?"

He released her. "I don't think you want to see it."

She straightened her spine. "I need to."

He shook his head. "It's pretty graphic. It bothered me and it'll be worse for you."

She grabbed his hand. "I need to know what I'm up against."

He dropped his shoulders. At least, he'd be here for her if she fell apart. "All right. What do you need to do?"

"I just need to touch your head." She placed her hands on each side of his head, temples to jaw, with her thumbs under his eyes. "Now think about what you saw in the premonition."

He didn't want to remember the horror, but did it for her.

***

Trill stared into his wary eyes. They were a striking pale blue and surrounded by dark lashes that were way thicker than they had any right to be. His face was so warm under her cool hands. She closed her eyes and her hands warmed with the connection. Resistance met her as she entered his thoughts. What he'd seen really had bothered him. She liked his energy, a bit confused, but true and good.

The dream began with her splayed out on her dining room table. Even though Adam already told her Art would kill the baby, seeing the huge knife in Art's hand sent protective fear coursing through her blood. Minutes ago, she'd learned about this child, and despite who the father was she already loved it. Disgust and anger filled her for the man who'd somehow coerced her into having sex with him so that he could create a baby to sacrifice.

In the premonition, her pregnant belly was bigger than at present, but couldn't be full term. Tammy had little Zach a couple of months ago and she'd been huge. Maybe it was more than a couple months ago. She didn't know if her whole recent world was like a dream or only the portions that included Art. Her friend might not know Trill was pregnant.

The symbols Art drew on the table weren't visible in her point of view. She probably wouldn't recognize them anyway, since they must enhance evil energy.

She cringed when Art carved into her belly. At least, he'd done something so she wouldn't feel the pain. Or maybe he'd done it so no one would hear her scream. She shivered.

The tiny baby dangled by a leg. A son. She needed to do whatever was necessary to protect him from this man who sired him. She wouldn't think of him as her child's father.

He cut the umbilical cord and chanted. She flinched as purple lightning licked her son's body, then coursed up Art's arms. He draped her child across her abdomen, cleaned up, then plunged the knife into her chest. She grunted and fell back from Adam, breaking their connection.

"Oh-my-god-oh-my-god. I can't believe he did that." She wiped the tears from her cheeks.

Adam clasped her hands. "I didn't want you to see it."

She sucked in a breath, held it for several seconds, then let it out. "I had to see what I was up against." She stood. "I have to get out of here."

She ran to her bedroom and Adam followed. He leaned against the doorframe as she tossed clothes on the bed. Maternity clothes. She didn't know where they'd come from. Did she function while she was under Art's control? She only had a few hazy memories, and they didn't include Art. Or being pregnant.

She grabbed a suitcase from her closet and stacked her clothes in it. From the bathroom she snatched up her toiletries, added them to her bag and zipped it closed. "Thanks so much for breaking the spell and telling me what Art was doing."

Adam picked up her bag. "Come on. Let's go."

"But you did your part already. I can't expect you to keep helping me."

He gripped her hand. "I can't leave you to fight this on your own, when he finds you. I'm involved because of the premonition. I have to help you."

The two brothers were so different. One protecting life, the other taking it.

She grabbed her purse from the dresser.

"You have to leave your phone or he might be able to track you."

She opened her purse, and didn't see her phone,

rummaged through the bottom, but didn't find it. She frowned. "I don't know where it is."

He shook his head. "Who leaves a pregnant woman with no means to call someone in an emergency?"

Not someone she wanted in her life. "Wait! I need to call work if I'm going to be gone."

Adam raised his eyebrows. "You really think you've been working? Art supplied you with groceries yesterday."

Her legs couldn't hold her and she leaned against the wall. She hadn't considered that she'd been non-functioning while she was under Art's control. It probably wasn't worth calling the school to find out when she last worked. She'd miss the kids, but they'd likely gotten a new aide months ago.

He held out his hand. "Come on. Let's get out of here."

They passed through the dining room and she picked up the flowers. Adam raised his brows.

"No one's ever given me flowers. I'm taking them." Even if he didn't know who she was when he bought them, and it was only a way to get into her house. "What about that?" She pointed at the necklace on the floor.

He shrugged. "I guess we should take it so Art wonders if you're still wearing it." He picked it up by the broken chain. "I'll throw it out down the road somewhere."

She stopped beside her car. "Should I take my car to let him think I left under my own power?"

"That's a good idea. You can park it in my garage."

A door opened behind her and she spun around.

Her neighbor hovered a few steps from the house. "Trill, is everything all right?"

Trill's shoulders sagged. "Hi, Mazy." She didn't know how much she should tell her friend or how much her friend knew. "Um…"

Adam stepped beside her and wrapped an arm around her waist, touching his forehead to her temple. "Honey, it's okay. It's probably best that she know." He faced Mazy. "Art's been abusive. I've known Trill for years, and she called me when Art hurt her. I'm taking her where he can't find her. I'd advise you to keep your door locked and don't talk to him."

Mazy hugged Trill. "I'm so sorry. I wish I'd known."

Trill touched her friend's shoulder. "There's nothing you could have done."

Mazy tipped her head. "You seem more yourself. I've been worried."

"Yeah, I feel better. I think he—"

"Was drugging her." Adam finished for her.

"Oh." Mazy patted Trill's tummy. "I hope that didn't harm the baby. You should call the police since he was harming both of you."

Adam tugged Trill closer. "We'll call the police and get her checked out. Now, we really have to leave."

Trill tugged away. "Wait. Mazy, do you know about my work?"

Her friend squinted. "What work? You haven't been there since—I don't know—you found out you were pregnant."

The words were a punch to her gut. She couldn't imagine what she'd done with her days for all these months. Sat on the couch in a stupor? She must have been able to feed herself. She couldn't imagine Art coming three times a day to make her eat. She drew in a breath. That was over. She needed to move on from here.

Adam touched her arm. "Trill, we have to leave before Art shows up."

Mazy took a step back. "Oh, yes. Of course. Be careful, Trill."

She grasped Mazy's hand.

"I will." She didn't know if she'd ever see her friend

again.

Adam helped her get into her car. She had to slide the seat back to fit in her tummy. Maybe she hadn't driven it lately. She fired up the engine as Adam strode to his car and tossed her suitcase into the back seat. In twenty minutes time, her life had been shredded.

Chapter 4

Adam glanced at Trill Song. A name as beautiful as the woman. She'd tipped the car seat back and been sleeping for about an hour. Her shiny, black hair spilled over the headrest. Even in repose, her serene face was nothing like the one he'd seen in the vision. In his premonition, her features had been slack, as if her consciousness had been buried deeper than normal sleep.

After leaving Trill's car in his garage, they'd stopped at his bank and he'd withdrawn two-thousand dollars in cash. With careful spending, it should be enough to see them through. At some point Art would figure out that he was with Trill.

His gaze flicked to the GPS. Only two miles left to their destination. He hoped this wasn't a bad decision. Trill didn't remember her time with Art, so she didn't know if she'd told him about her grandmother who lived within the Wampanoag reservation in Mashpee. They were taking a chance coming to her, but Trill felt strongly that they needed to.

He completed the last turn and rubbed Trill's arm. "Hey, honey, we're almost there." It just slipped out. In front of Mazy, he wanted to give the impression that they were very good friends, but now, calling her honey warmed him.

She stretched and tipped the back of the seat up, then rolled her head. "Already? I didn't expect to fall asleep." She pointed ahead and to the left. "There. The green house."

He turned into the driveway of a small ranch-style house, and parked beside a beat up white Corolla. Four-foot tall evergreen bushes grew at each corner of the house, and mulched, empty flowerbeds waited for spring to rouse them to life.

Trill jumped from the car and ran up the steps at the side of the house. She knocked twice on the door and threw it open. "Gram?"

Adam followed her, and waited in the doorway.

A gray haired woman, a head shorter than Trill entered the kitchen from a hallway, a smile on her face.

"Trillium, I've been worried. You haven't returned my calls. I'd finally convinced Wolf to go check up on you. And what's this?" She patted the woman's belly, and glared at Adam.

He hadn't expected that Trill was a nickname. He loved her full name, and it suited her.

"Gram, Adam saved my life." Trill hugged the older woman. "I'm in so much trouble." With one arm still around her grandmother, Trill twisted around and held out a hand to Adam. He stepped forward and clasped it.

"Gram, this is Adam. This morning, he rescued me from his brother, Art. Adam, this is my wonderful grandmother, Freesia."

"Nice to meet you, Freesia."

The older woman's hand was warm and dry. She stared at him for a few seconds, then gathered him into a hug. It had been way too many years since he'd had a grandmother hug. She released him and wrapped an arm around her granddaughter. "Let's go sit down and you can tell me what's going on."

They sat on a comfortable, brown couch, with Trill in the center. The furnishings in the small room were worn, but well cared for. Tabletops and the wooden floor gleamed. Adam's gaze skimmed several family photos on the wall. Trill, when she was nine or ten, stared into the face of a boy. They looked enough alike that he had to be her brother or cousin.

Freesia took Trill's hand. "Tell me what's going on and why I haven't heard from you in months."

As Trill filled her in, Freesia's browned skin paled, making her appear to be a frail old woman. Adam hated the reminder of Art's plot for Trill, but it had to be so much worse for the grandmother who loved her.

Freesia reached across Trill and squeezed Adam's hand. "Thank you, son, for saving my girl's life."

"You're welcome. But I don't think she's out of danger yet. Art will try to find her."

"How did you end up with a brother like him?"

He shook his head. "I think it goes the other way. How did Art end up with a brother like me? He's like our father."

"You're a good man, Adam." Freesia gave her granddaughter a stern stare. "Trill, why did you come here? Won't this Art guy look for you with family?"

Trill bit her lip. "I don't know what he knows. But, Gram. I had to come."

Adam didn't like the sadness in Trill's voice.

"I can't feel the baby's spirit. I need you to check it for me."

Trill had mentioned not liking Art's energy, and Adam wondered if that was the same as a spirit. His must have been better than his brother's since she'd accompanied him.

The woman slid to the floor and settled in front of Trill. She placed a hand on each side of Trill's belly, closed her eyes, and began to hum.

Several minutes passed. It didn't seem like it should take this long to sense the baby's spirit. Trill's hand clenched. Adam closed his over it and she turned hers, gripping his fingers.

Freesia lifted her gaze to Trill, sadness in her eyes. “I sense no spirit in this child. I’ve never come across this before.”

Trill’s hand twitched. “He can’t be born without a spirit.” She placed a protective hand over her stomach, and her eyes widened. “Does that mean he was supposed to die like Adam predicted, so he doesn’t need a spirit? Was I supposed to die, too?”

“No.” Adam snatched his hand from hers and wrapped his arm around her shoulders. He didn’t know why it bothered him so much to think of her dying. They’d known each other less than twelve hours.

Trill grasped her grandmother’s hands. “Is there anything we can do?”

Freesia struggled to stand, and Adam jumped up to help her. She resumed her place beside Trill. The wrinkles at the corners of her eyes were more pronounced as she stared at Trill. “I’ll consult the ancestors, and see what they have to say.” She patted her granddaughter’s leg. “In the meantime, why don’t you help me with dinner while this young man brings in your bags?” She stood and pointed down the hall. “The first door on the right is Trillium’s. You may use the first on the left.”

***

Trill woke slowly. Her old room. She hadn’t lived in it since before college, but she visited weekends every couple of months. With the hazy months-long gap, she didn’t know when she’d visited last or if she’d called Gram.

She struggled out of bed. Probably, if she remembered getting bigger day-by-day, she would have adapted. Despite being so large, she found it hard to believe she was pregnant.

She'd always imagined her babies being conceived with love, not because of a twisted man's need of a sacrifice. No child deserved a start like that, and she'd do her best to make sure he didn't end like that either.

She showered, dressed, and headed for the kitchen.

Adam sat at the table, a plate of pancakes and sausage in front of him. Gram flipped a pancake. A stack sat beside the stove.

Trill yawned. Maybe she should have stayed in bed longer. She didn't know how much sleep she should get. "Morning."

Adam pulled out the chair beside him. "Have a seat."

She sat and Gram put a plate before her and a glass of orange juice.

"Gram, I should have made you breakfast." Her first morning home, she always made breakfast.

Gram glanced at Trill's belly. "You need more sleep than you used to."

"I guess." She rubbed her belly. It itched. "This is so crazy. It's like I got dropped into someone else's body. I opened the closet door and my belly got in the way." If she'd been in a rush, she'd probably have bruises. "And I don't know how far along I am. I don't even know if I've been to a doctor."

Freesia flipped a pancake. "You should probably go. Maybe he can guess on a due date, and make sure everything's all right."

"But it's not all right. This baby's just a shell with no spirit."

Gram patted her hand and sat down with her own plate. "We're going to fix that after breakfast."

Her heart soared. She'd known about the baby for less than a day, but she wanted the best for him. "The ancestors talked to you?"

Her grandmother gave a gentle smile. "Yes. There's no spirit because the one he was conceived with was evil. Your energy forced it to leave."

"Wow. I wonder if I sensed that in my hazy world." She didn't know her power could do something on its own, without her direction. Maybe she'd consciously done it, sensing the evil spirit and actively gotten rid of it. Maybe not. Thinking about it now, she would probably have been afraid to tamper with the spirit, in case it killed the baby, but with the clouded state she'd been in, it might not have mattered to her.

Gram picked up her fork and sliced through a sausage patty. "The ancestors have promised that there's a good strong spirit waiting to enter your baby, and they told me how to get them together."

"Oh, Gram." Tears brimmed her eyes. Her baby would have a strong spirit, one chosen specifically for him. He'd be even less a part of the evil man who'd helped conceive him. She could love this child, knowing the ancestors had made him special.

Adam took her hand. "See. Everything's going to be fine."

While they ate, Trill caught up on the local news. She usually enjoyed visiting with friends when she visited, but she wasn't looking forward to explaining what had happened to her.

Gram stood. "Let's get started." They all cleared the table, putting the dishes in the sink.

Her grandmother retrieved an oval dish from the kitchen counter, with twisted dry grass draped across it, and set it on the edge of the table. She lit one end of the grass with a match, and the scent of sweet grass and sage swirled into the air. She turned two chairs so their backs were to the table. "Trillium, you sit here." She touched the top of the closest chair. "And Adam, sit beside her."

Trill suspected why Gram was involving Adam in the ceremony, but wasn't sure it was a good idea.

Gram knelt in front of Trill. "You two join hands."

Adam raised his eyebrows, shrugged and took her hand.

Gram placed her hands on Trill's thighs and closed her eyes. She began to chant in Wampanoag.

As a child, Trill had spoken the language, but now, she only understood a few words. She closed her eyes, and let herself become immersed in the song. The tension that had tightened her muscles since waking from Art's spell left her. Her shoulders relaxed and the pressure in her head eased. Every breath of incense she drew in filled a void she hadn't known was empty. A warm breeze touched her cheek and swirled her hair. She breathed it in. The warmth entered her lungs and slid down. The little life inside her twitched as the spirit entered its new home.

She startled when pressure touched her belly, and her eyes popped open, finding her grandmother scooting back from kissing her belly. She grinned at Trill. "It's done. Your son has a wonderful spirit."

Trill laid a hand on each side of her tummy and drew in the essence of the new spirit. Love flowed into her and she couldn't help but reciprocate. Disgust no longer filled her at being impregnated by an evil man. This child's new spirit was strong and true, and she would do everything necessary to make sure he stayed safe.

Adam helped Freesia stand. "I felt something touch me. It reminded me of my mother's touch."

She squeezed his forearm. "The spirit was getting to know you."

He frowned. "Why?"

"Because you will be important to him."

His eyebrows rose. Trill wondered about that, too.

Chapter 5

On their fourth day visiting Trill's grandmother, Trill had an obstetrical appointment. Freesia had informed Trill the day before that she already had plans for that time and couldn't take her. Adam figured Trill didn't want a near stranger along on the doctor's visit, so offered to let Trill take his car. She didn't want to go alone, which could be a bad idea anyway, since they didn't know when Art might show up. Of course, he accompanied her.

He sat beside her in the doctor's waiting room. She paged through a baby magazine and his gaze passed over the two other pregnant women in the room. They were probably excited about becoming mothers, maybe had planned their pregnancies. Trill certainly wasn't unique in having an unplanned pregnancy, but having to run for her life from the father had to be.

A nurse stepped into the room, holding a chart. "Trillium Song?"

Trill struggled to her feet.

"Please come with me."

He figured he'd wait out here for her, but the worry in her eyes drew him to his feet. In her mind, she'd been pregnant a few days, not months. A hundred things could be wrong without her knowing it, and she had no one else.

He took her hand and she gave a tentative smile.

The nurse weighed Trill on a scale in the hallway and led them to an exam room. She had Trill climb onto the exam table, and took her blood pressure. He stood beside her as the nurse asked a slew of questions, and frowned several times when Trill couldn't answer basic questions about the last few months. He placed a hand on her shoulder, and she glanced at him. What woman wouldn't know if she'd been to the doctor since she got pregnant? Or if she'd been eating right. Or had morning sickness.

The nurse closed the chart. "The doctor will be with you in a few minutes."

"Do you still want me to stay?"

She bit her lip, nodding.

He sat in the chair near the head of the exam table.

The doctor walked in with the chart under her arm. She was shorter than Trill, and had short, dark, curly hair, and might have some Native American heritage. She held out her hand to Trill. "I'm Dr. Montgomery."

"Trill Song. And this is Adam Richards."

He shook the doctor's hand.

"You're the father?"

"Yes." He answered quickly, before Trill could. He didn't hesitate, knowing that if he'd said no, the doctor might have made him leave. Trill wanted him there, so he hoped she didn't mind.

She raised her eyebrows, and he shrugged. They should have discussed all these issues before coming in, except he thought he'd be staying in the waiting room.

"Dad, you can sit there." She pointed to the chair he'd vacated, and opened the folder. "We have some missing history."

Adam leaned forward. "She had a few months of amnesia."

Dr. Montgomery studied Trill. "Amnesia?"

Trill stared at her hands. "I was sort of in a trance. I don't remember anything from that time."

The doctor glared at him. He lifted his hands. "It wasn't me. I rescued her from it." He realized he may have created a trap. It didn't make sense that he was the baby's father, but not responsible for Trill's amnesia.

The doctor glanced from one to the other. "You should see a neurologist about the amnesia episode in case there's permanent damage."

Trill nodded. "I will. I didn't realize it might have caused more harm."

Dr. Montgomery wrote on her chart. "I'll have Darcy give you his number."

Adam didn't think Trill would make that appointment.

The doctor set the folder on the counter, and picked up a wand device, coating the end with a clear gel. "We'll listen for the baby's heartbeat first. Lie back, Trill. Lift your shirt." The doctor pushed Trill's pants below her belly. She touched the wand to Trill's tummy, slid it around, and held it in place when a shushing beat started on the monitor. "That's the baby's heartbeat. It sounds perfect."

Adam grabbed Trill's hand. He didn't expect to be excited about it. The baby was his nephew, but hearing the proof of the little life swelled his heart with love. In his premonition, he'd seen the little guy, but his only thought had been to save his and his mother's lives. Now, he wanted more than to keep this child safe, he wanted to be a part of the child's life.

He gazed at Trill's face. Her eyes wide, staring at her stomach, a hint of a smile on her lips. She flicked her gaze to him and they seemed to make some kind of connection.

The doctor set the wand on the counter, silencing the heartbeat, then wrote on the chart. "Let's do the rest of the exam." She listened to Trill's heart and lungs, took some measurements, and a few other things, then rested her hands on her knees. "I'll set up an ultrasound for tomorrow. It's especially important since you don't have a previous record of any problems you might have."

Trill scooted off the table. "Dr. Montgomery, thank you for seeing me so quickly."

Adam followed Trill out of the office, incredibly pleased that she'd allowed him to participate in the introduction to her baby.

***

Trill glanced at Adam as he found a parking space in front of the same building they'd been at the day before.

It seemed natural when he took her hand to help her from the car. She was a bit nervous about the ultrasound. She didn't have a memory of seeing a doctor, but then the vision of her baby dangling from Art's hand came to mind. Her son had looked perfect, except he was too small. She shivered from the conclusion of the premonition where Art had draped her weakened son over her lifeless body.

Adam stopped and frowned. "Are you okay?"

"Mostly. I just had a flash of that vision of yours."

He wrapped an arm around her shoulder, buddy fashion. "I wished you hadn't asked to see it. I don't want you to have a memory of your son like that."

She nodded, wishing she could wipe that vision from her brain. "I know, but I might not have agreed to leave without seeing the reason."

His hand caressed her back for a few more seconds, then he stepped away. "We better get inside or we'll be late. Thanks for letting me accompany you."

Her baby had a chance at life because of Adam. She couldn't deny him this. Not that she understood why he wanted to be there. Yes, he was the baby's uncle, but he seemed more invested in it than that.

The doors swished open as they approached. It was a different entrance than the one they'd used the day before. She stopped at a directory sign in the entry, and found the ultrasound department on the first floor of the two story hospital.

Adam pointed to their left. "That way."

They walked side-by-side, and entered the door marked *Ultrasound.*

A young woman glanced up as she tucked a paper covering over the bottom of the exam table. "Trillium Song?"

"Yes."

"You're just in time. Come on over, and we can get started."

Trill handed Adam her purse.

The tech patted the table. "Hop on up." She swept past them and swished a curtain across the room to block the view from the door, then returned to her instruments. She adjusted some dials, and held up the transducer. "All right, lie back and bare the belly."

Trill giggled and did as ordered. She held her hand out to Adam, suddenly afraid of what the scan would show. She'd seen the baby in Adam's premonition, and he'd appeared normal, but now she was afraid something would be wrong with him. She tried to convince herself that the spirit wouldn't have gone into him if he wouldn't survive. Maybe every mother had a fear that her baby would have a problem.

The tech placed the cold, gooey transducer against Trill's stomach. "Do you want to know the sex of the baby?"

"It's a boy," Adam responded instantly.

Trill glanced at him in surprise, and he shrugged. Maybe he hadn't meant to say it.

The tech chuckled. "Most daddies want boys, but we'll

see."

Again Adam had been mistaken for the baby's father and didn't flinch.

Movement on the screen caught her attention. A little arm and hand, the fingers curled. The view changed as the tech skimmed over Trill's belly. Every so often, she snapped a picture. This was so much better than the vision. The body wasn't as clear, but she didn't feel the horror of when her child was tortured by the lightning and left to die.

She glanced at Adam, his gaze was trained on the screen, a small smile lit his face. He seemed more mesmerized than her. She turned her attention back to the screen as the baby's sex appeared on the screen.

The tech chuckled. "Yes, this is a boy." She slid the transducer to the far side, giving them a view of a leg as the baby kicked.

A little flutter corresponded to the movement. Now she could associate them with the baby's action.

A printer whirred and the tech handed Adam two sheets of paper. He held one in each hand, staring at them, a smile lighting up his face. He glowed like a proud father. If only he was and not his brother. Her life would be so much different if she'd met Adam first.

***

Adam shoved his cell phone in his pocket and from the kitchen table grabbed the insulated lunch bag Trill had prepared.

"Come on, Adam." Trill stood at the open door, sunshine streaming around her. She'd called the reservation school the day before and asked if she could help out. Her eyes sparkled with excitement. She missed working with children.

This would be a new experience for him. The last time

he'd done anything with kids was when he was a kid himself, but he didn't dare leave her alone. There was no telling if or when Art would show up.

As he approached, Trill strode down the walk and passed his car.

He caught up and grabbed her arm. "Hold on. We're taking the car."

She tipped her head. "It's only three blocks. I walked every day when I was a kid."

He steered her to the passenger door. "You didn't have to worry about Art back then. If he shows up, it's better if we have transportation."

Trill lowered herself into the seat. "Fine." She'd lost some of her excitement.

At the school, students milled in the hallways, and Trill waded through them with him behind her. The secretary directed them to a third grade classroom.

They stepped into the room and the teacher's eyes widened, focused on Trill's belly. "Trill, I didn't know."

"Hi, Beck." She hugged the woman, and stepped back. "It was a surprise for me, too. Becky Stone, this is Adam Richards, my baby's uncle."

They shook hands. "In front of the children, I'm Mrs. Stone. You'll be Mr. Richards. Trill, are you still Miss Song?"

"Yes."

Children streamed into the classroom and took seats. They whispered to each other and stared at the newcomers.

Becky faced the students. "Today Mr. Richards and Miss Song are going to work with some of you."

One of the boys stared at him. "Is she having your baby?"

Adam's face warmed. He hadn't expected kids to be so direct.

Trill gripped his upper arm. "Mr. Richards is my baby's uncle."

He hoped the family connection satisfied them.

Becky sat at her desk. "Let me take roll, then we'll break up into reading groups." She made a couple checks in her book, then stood and pointed to a corner in the back of the room. "All right, bears over there." She pointed at the other back corner. "Wolves there, and coyotes in this front corner."

Children scampered to their places and sat in three circles, their eyes on Becky.

"Max, Faun, and Tommy, can you get the books for your group? Be sure to count how many and get one for the teacher."

One child from each circle stood, counted the students surrounding them and ran to stacks of books on a shelf. Two of the students carried the same books back to their group, but the coyotes group had a different book.

Becky gazed at Adam. "Mr. Richards, can you take the coyotes group?" She lowered her voice. "They're my advanced students. I have a feeling you'll do better with them. Have each of them read one page. Miss Song, you can have the bears."

Adam sat in the empty space between a girl and boy. "So, what are we reading?" He picked up the book from the floor in front of him, a gorilla and elephant on the cover.

"Ivan!" the kids chorused together.

"Shh-shh." Adam glanced over his shoulder, reminded of when he was a kid and had done something wrong in class. Some of the kids had their books open part way through, so they weren't starting from the beginning. This time he pointed to a girl. "What page are we on?"

"Thirty-six." A sweet little voice, not loud enough to disturb the whole class.

Adam scanned the group. "When it's your turn, tell me

your name and then read a page." He glanced down at the girl beside him. "We'll start with you."

Her big brown eyes stared into his. "Shania." She dropped her head to her book and started to read.

Each child took a turn, and Adam rarely had to give assistance or correct a word. They were a smart bunch of kids and the story was actually fun. The other groups were still reading. "Let's go round again."

The last child was halfway through his page when Becky called out. "All right, stack your books and get back into your seats." The children who had retrieved the books returned them to the shelf.

Trill and Adam helped individual students with math and English, then they had a break with Becky when the children had lunch and went outside for recess.

Adam silently ate his sandwich while Trill caught up with Becky.

Becky glanced at him and back to Trill. "Why are you with Adam and not the baby's father?"

Trill bit her lip. "I'm not really with Adam. He's…sort of my protector from his brother."

It stung a little. What she said was totally true, but Adam was more than her protector.

Becky's eyes widened. "He was abusive?"

"You could say that."

"What did—"

"I don't want to talk about it. Tell me how everybody's doing, in case I don't get to see them."

They talked about Trill's friends, and Adam felt left out, but enjoyed watching her have fun with Becky, seeing the friendship they shared. He didn't have those kinds of friends. Trill laughed a lot and he wondered if that was her normal when she wasn't running for her life.

Maybe someday he could give that to her.

Chapter 6

Adam woke, a heavy pounding in his head. Something was wrong. They'd been at Freesia's for nine days without his brother making an appearance. Maybe he'd given up—unlikely since he'd invested so much in Trill.

Adam had been thinking the past few days he should leave. He helped out when he could, but they didn't need him, and Trill seemed safe enough, but the thought of never seeing her again saddened him. Her smiles, her thoughts on so many subjects, the occasional brush of her hand. Even never seeing her intuitive grandmother bothered him.

Adam gripped his head, the pain intensifying. He stood and his senses were assaulted with images. He fell back to the bed and let the premonition take over.

***

Adam stood in the hallway outside his bedroom, the vision giving him a feeling of being in his surroundings, but not a part of them. He headed down the hall to Freesia's kitchen. Most mornings, Freesia and Trill's voices drifted down the hall, and coffee cups clinked as they were set on the table. Silence meant they weren't up yet, or something was wrong. Impending doom thrummed in his chest. Something familiar squeaked but he couldn't place it.

He stepped into the kitchen and froze. Freesia lay on the

floor near the table, her head in a pool of blood. Adam sprawled on the far side of the table, his hands and feet bound by rope. At least his brother didn't want him dead. The same couldn't be said for Trill.

She lay on the kitchen table, her legs dangling from the knees over the edge, her ankles bound. Her arms stretched over her head and were tied to the back of a chair.

Her fearful eyes widened when he stepped into view around Art's back, and Adam stumbled. He'd never had a premonition where one of the subjects could see him observing.

She no longer wore Art's controlling necklace and he must have opted to not make this easy for her by knocking her out. He could have done it with some herbs and a spell.

"I'm sorry. I can't help." He punched his fist through Art's back to demonstrate his impotence. He almost wished this future Trill didn't know he was there, watching and letting her go through this torture. It wasn't real. The real Trill wasn't experiencing it, but her fear was all too real for him.

Art drew symbols on the maple table using a black marker.

Adam rushed to Trill's side and squatted down. If only he could touch her to help her in some way. He tried to caress her face, but his hand passed through it. There was nothing he could do to protect her in the premonition.

"Baby, look at me. I can't stop Art. I can't stop the pain you're going to feel, but keep your eyes on me and I'll try to be a distraction." The fear and tears broke his heart. "We're in a premonition. This feels real to you, but it's not. I'm sorry. As soon as I wake, I'm getting you and your grandmother out of here. It's not going to happen. I won't let it."

She gasped and her gaze flashed to Art. He'd started to

cut into her abdomen. He hated that she experienced this pain, and soon would experience the emotional pain of seeing her son die.

"No, baby, look at me." He cringed inside each time she whimpered or writhed in pain. "Think about something else. Like helping the kids at school. You got right down with them and taught them those songs. Can you sing—"

At the weak cry, they swiveled their heads, seeing the small infant in Art's hands. He ached at Trill's desperate cry. From viewing his previous premonition, she knew how this would end. During the other vision, he'd wanted to help the unconscious woman and her child, but this time, he cared about them. The baby was already a part of his life. Even though the vision wasn't real, and he might again be able to prevent it, Trill's pain tore him up.

Art finished his ritual as the last of the purple lightning faded.

"Trill!"

She turned her gaze back to him.

"Beg him not to kill you. He's got what he wants. Maybe you can stop the rest." He couldn't state what the rest was, but she knew.

Her watery gaze found Adam's brother. "Art! You got your power. Please, don't kill the baby and me. Give us a chance."

Art draped the baby over her. "The ritual isn't finished. I've got to spill the blood of the mother."

Trill closed her eyes and they shot open. "You did that when you took the baby from me. Isn't that enough?"

He lifted the knife. "I don't know. I'm not taking any chances of it reversing." He plunged the knife into her chest.

Adam couldn't stop the tears from spilling down his cheeks. He couldn't imagine that his father had planned this for Jamie, the girl Adam was supposed to love his whole life.

Would his father have allowed her to give birth, then done the ritual and killed her? Adam was grateful her boyfriend and family had rescued her.

Now, it was his turn to rescue Trill, no matter what it took.

***

Adam came out of the trance with the image of Trill's staring, dead eyes in his mind. He'd do everything in his power to keep her safe. He groaned and his door flew open, slamming against the wall.

Trill raced across the floor and squatted next to him. "Adam, what's wrong?"

She reached toward him and he batted her hands away. He didn't want her to see this premonition. The last one was bad enough. This one included her grandmother dead on the floor.

He sat up. "I had another premonition. We're getting out of here as soon as we get packed. Freesia's coming, too. Does she have somewhere she can stay?"

If Freesia was home alone when Art showed up, he'd kill her if she wouldn't tell him where to find Trill.

"When is he getting here?"

He glanced away. "I don't know, but soon." He'd thought about leaving, and if he had, it wouldn't have been far off. Since he'd been in the vision, it had to be before that.

He stood and helped Trill to her feet.

She stepped back. "All right. I'll go tell Gram."

He dressed quickly, stuffed his dirty clothes beside the clean in his bag, and carried it to the back door and dropped it. He leaned against the jam, and stared down the hall. Trill stepped out first, her bag wheeling behind her. She waited beside him, worry in her eyes.

A few moments later, Freesia appeared, a bag slung over her shoulder and a rifle in her hands.

He straightened away from the wall. "A gun?"

She glared. "Did you expect a bow and arrows?"

He laughed. "I'm not sure what good it will do. Is it even loaded?"

"Of course, it is. You don't haul out a gun unless you're ready to use it."

He picked up his bag, and held out his hand to Freesia.

She stepped back, and frowned.

He bent his fingers. "I'll take your bag. You keep the gun."

She handed the bag over. He headed out the door, and opened the trunk, dropping the two bags inside. Trill's suitcase thumped down the steps and he scooped it up and placed it beside the others.

An engine rumbled down the street and his blood chilled at the sight of Art's BMW. "In the car! Now!" He thrust his keys into Trill's hand. "In the driver's seat. I'm going to try to delay him, so you and Freesia can get out of here."

"I can't leave you." Her eyes widened.

He rubbed her belly. "You have to protect your son."

She bit her lip, got into the car, and started it.

Freesia stood beside the car, her gun pointed down the driveway, as the black car barreled toward them.

"Freesia, get in the car." Trill wouldn't leave without her grandmother. He wanted to shove her inside and slam the door closed, but he was afraid he'd hurt the woman, or her gun might go off.

"He wants to kill my granddaughter and great-grandson. I would be justified if I shot him."

As much as he hated his brother right now, Adam didn't want him dead.

Art stopped two feet behind Adam's car, and jumped

out. “Imagine meeting you here, big brother.” He took a couple of steps forward.

Freesia lifted her gun higher. “Stop right there!”

Art froze. “I came to get what’s mine. Drop the gun, old lady, before I hurt you.” He raised his hand.

Freesia lifted her chin. “How are you going to do that without a gun?”

“Like this.” Art slowly curled his outstretched fingers and thumb.

Freesia gagged and her color darkened. Her arms trembled. She squeezed off a shot that hit Art in the shin. He screamed and his hold on Freesia broke. She shot again, tearing a hole in one of the BMW’s tires.

Art clutched his leg. “Stop, bitch!” He lifted his hand and squeezed. The pain must have messed up his power because Freesia seemed unaffected this time.

Freesia yanked a car door open, and fell into the seat. “Let’s go.”

Adam threw himself into the front seat.

Trill coughed, and hit the gas, driving behind the house and around the far side. She took in gasping breaths. It was Trill Art had tried to choke the second time, but she’d driven out of his range. She tore across the snowy yard and bounced up onto the road.

She was amazing. Even through Art’s attack, she persevered and did what she needed to do.

Adam glanced back. Art sat on the ground, one hand over his leg, blood flowing between his fingers, the other holding his phone. He screamed. “You can’t hide from me. I’ll find you.”

Adam’s gaze settled on Freesia. “That was some fine shooting.”

She grinned. “Who do you think taught Trillium and Wolf how to shoot?”

His brows rose and he glanced at Trill. "You can shoot?"

She nodded. "Rifle and handgun. I'm pretty good, too. Not as good as Wolf though. And I hate hunting. I cried when I shot my first rabbit, and that was it for me."

They crossed a small highway. Adam figured Trill would have turned onto it since they could go faster than on this rural road. "Are you going somewhere in particular, or just putting distance between us and Art?"

Freesia dropped her head back and closed her eyes. "She's going to Wolf's. I can stay there for a few days while the two of you find someplace to hide."

That made sense. If Art tracked Trill, it would put Freesia in danger again if she stayed with Wolf. If Art knew about Wolf, hopefully, he'd give up if Trill wasn't there, or else Wolf could keep his grandmother safe. Well, maybe they'd keep each other safe.

Now, Adam needed to figure out where Trill would be safe. He didn't know if Art had found her because he knew of her grandmother, or if he used a find spell. She had an apartment full of belongings he could use for a spell, but Trill also carried Art's baby. He might be able to track his own child, which meant Trill wasn't safe anywhere.

He glanced at Trill's grandmother. "Freesia, do you know a way to block someone from tracking another person? I'm afraid that Art tracked Trill through the baby."

Freesia waved a hand. "I'll talk to the ancestors. Now that they've provided a spirit for the baby, they'll want to protect it." She closed her eyes again.

He wasn't used to being a passenger, and didn't know how long it would take to get to Wolf's house. "Trill, do you want me to drive?"

She glanced at him. "No, I'm fine driving. I'd have to tell you all the turns to make." She narrowed her eyes. "Unless you don't want me to drive."

"I was just concerned about you being pregnant."

Her eyebrows rose. "I'm not an invalid, but if I had to be in the driver's seat for hours, it might get uncomfortable. It's just another half-hour."

With Trill driving, Adam had a chance to watch her. In such a short time, she'd come to mean so much to him. The spirit's touch, before entering the baby, had left him with a longing to be the child's father. If Trill knew, she'd probably think he was trying to control her life in a different way than his brother. Adam was somewhat surprised that she let him, the brother of the man who wanted to kill her, be her protector. She trusted him to not want her dead.

Trill waited at a traffic light before taking a right onto a busy street. A cell phone store caught his attention. Now that Art knew that Adam was with Trill, he might try to track his phone. "Pull into that parking lot."

She frowned, but took a quick turn, into an empty space. "Why?"

"I need to get a phone Art can't trace. We'll get you one, too." He glanced into the back seat. "That way your grandmother can call you."

The women stayed in the car while he bought the phones. He returned with a bag, and assembled the phones, adding each other's phone numbers to them. He opened the address book on his regular phone and started adding numbers he might need. Once done, he popped the back off his old phone, removed the battery, and dropped them into the glove box. He slipped his new phone in his pocket, and dropped Trill's into her open purse, on the floor beside his feet.

"Let's get going." They'd already spent too long in the open, even though Art would be incapacitated for a while yet.

A few minutes later, Trill took a left into an apartment complex. He'd expected Wolf to live in a cabin in the woods.

"Wolf lives here?"

Trill chuckled. "Surprising, isn't it?" She pointed to the back of the parking lot and the woods beyond. "There's a trailhead over there and miles of hiking trails. He can't hunt there, but he can get close to nature."

They piled out of the car. Adam lifted Freesia's bag from the trunk and followed the women inside. Freesia received a surprised expression from a couple leaving the building. He might have done the same, passing an old woman carrying a rifle.

They climbed the stairs to the second floor and Trill knocked on the second door on the right. Wolf's windows would overlook the woods. After a handful of seconds, the door didn't open and Trill knocked harder. Still no answer.

Trill frowned. "I saw his truck in the lot. "Maybe he's hiking." She fished her hand to the bottom of her purse, and seemed to chase small objects. She grinned. "Here they are." She held up a key ring with two keys. One was a Ford key, probably for Wolf's truck. She inserted the other key into the door lock, twisted and pushed the door open.

They entered a living room, and he inspected it. "He's not going to be upset we let ourselves in?" A big screen TV hung on the wall and a deep cushioned forest green couch sat before it.

Trill dropped her purse beside the couch. "Nah. I'm going to make lunch." She disappeared through a door.

Adam's brother would probably beat him to a pulp if he entered Art's house without being invited. It must be nice to have the kind of relationship that allowed this.

He trailed the women into the kitchen and sat at the table. It wasn't a large room, maybe six feet of counter space.

Trill was no longer in the kitchen, but a few moments later, came down the hall toward him. Ah. Bathroom. He hadn't been around pregnant women before, but everybody knew their bladders got squashed.

Freesia had lined up deli meat and cheese on the counter with lettuce, condiments and bread. He half expected Freesia to take a venison roast from the refrigerator and cut thin slices.

Trill handed him a can of Coke. “Do you want a glass?”

He tipped the can. “This is fine.” He sat at the square table with his back to the wall.

Trill poured a glass of milk, and turned on the burner under the tea kettle.

After the women made sandwiches and Freesia poured hot water into her teacup, they took their seats, Freesia across from him and Trill on his right.

They were halfway through the meal when the door flew open, and slammed against the wall. From where he sat, Adam couldn’t see who had come in. He jackknifed out of his chair and jumped into the kitchen doorway, blocking anyone from getting to the women. He hoped.

A tall, broad-shouldered man with Trill’s chin and dark eyes stalked towards him. Adam half expected the man to wear braids, but his hair was fairly short, barely to the collar. Wolf leaned forward. “Who the hell are you?”

Trill peeked around Adam’s arm. “Hi, Wolf.”

Wolf’s gaze darted between the two of them. Scowling, he placed his hands on his hips. Yeah, wait until he got a glimpse of Trill.

Freesia’s voice drifted from behind them. “Let’s all sit down.”

Wolf’s head snapped to the right. “Gram? What are you guys doing here?”

Adam backed up, bumping into Trill’s belly.

Two long strides brought Wolf into the room. He snagged Trill’s arm and hauled her out from behind Adam. His eyes widened. “What the…”

He released Trill and grabbed the front of Adam's shirt with both fists. "What did you do to my sister?" He glanced at her. "I don't see you for months, and this is how you turn up?"

Trill bumped Wolf with her hip. "He's not the father, and he saved my life twice. Now, let him go."

Wolf opened his hands, placed them flat on Adam's chest and shoved. "How?"

Freesia slapped her hand on the table. "Wolf, make yourself a sandwich, and let's all sit down."

Freesia hadn't stood. He and Trill resumed their places, and Wolf took the remaining seat across from Trill without making a lunch.

Trill stretched across the table and Wolf took her hand. "Wolf, this is Adam Richards. He found out his brother was going to kill me, and rescued me." She explained everything, including their harrowing morning flight.

Throughout the explanation, Wolf shook. "He raped you," he rasped out.

"Well, not re—"

Wolf pounded the table. "Without the spell, you never would have seen him again. It was like giving you a date rape drug, only more effective. In my book, that's rape."

Trill's devastated expression cut him deep, and Adam wished he could take Trill into his arms. She hadn't thought of it like that, but it was true. Given a choice, she wouldn't have had sex with Art. And heaped on that criminal act, his brother wanted to murder her and the child he'd forced on her.

She gulped a couple of times and drew in a long breath, then straightened her shoulders. That was his Trill. She was ready to deal with their current problem.

Adam was relieved that Trill had ejected out the original spirit. In his mind, the new spirit took away any right Art had to this child. It was no longer a part of him. With the way the spirit had touched Adam before entering the baby, this child had become his own.

Wolf crossed his arms, and glared at Adam. "Do you have a plan?"

Adam shook his head. "Not really. Up to this point I've pretty much been reacting to my premonitions." He ran a hand through his hair. "I'm not some kind of secret agent. I don't know how to stay hidden from someone." His gaze sought out Trill. "I don't know how long you need to hide from my brother. I don't know if he needs to take the baby from your body for his ritual or if he can do it after he's born. I don't know if there's a finite time it needs to be done."

Wolf's gaze met his, studying him like a specimen. Not surprising considering they were talking about his sister's life. "Why are you involved in this? Why do you want to save her?"

Adam jabbed his own chest "These are my premonitions. They were sent to me for a reason. Whether it's to prevent Art from getting this power or to keep Trill alive, my goal is to keep Trill and her baby safe."

He hadn't answered the why. He didn't know. He could have delivered Trill to her grandmother and drove away, having done his part to save her life. If he'd done that, she would have died this morning. The image of her dead eyes staring at him wrenched his heart. Maybe that was the answer. He needed her to be alive because he cared for her.

Wolf glared. "If the reason is to prevent your brother from gaining power, you could kill the baby and be done with it."

Another pain wrenched his heart. "No! I'm going to do everything I can to keep this baby and his mother safe."

Wolf's expression softened when he gazed at his sister. He took her hand. "Trill, you could have an abortion and end

Art's reason to kill you. You've only known you were pregnant for a few days."

Her eyes widened and she sucked in a breath. She tore her hand from Wolf's and rubbed her belly with both hands. "Wolf, the ancestors granted him a spirit. I can't end that. Besides, I love him already."

Wolf let out a long breath and scrubbed his forehead. "Yeah, I didn't think you'd go for it." He leaned forward, forearms on the table. "So, let's make a plan." He glanced at Freesia. "The easy part is that Gram stays here until this is resolved."

Freesia nodded. "And I have to make a medicine bag for Trill in hopes it will cloud that man's ability to find her."

Wolf nodded. "Good idea, but I don't have much here."

"I have what I need."

She hadn't grabbed any herbs on her way through the kitchen. There must have been a stash in her bedroom, along with the guns she'd brought.

Wolf leaned forward. "You're blood relation to this baby, too. What's to say you don't decide to sacrifice him for your own power?"

Anger heated Adam's blood, and he leaped to his feet. "Seriously? If that's what I wanted to do, I could have performed the ritual at her apartment when I found her." He jabbed Wolf's chest. "I went there to save her."

Freesia slapped the table. "Adam, sit. He just wants to provoke you."

He dropped into his chair and crossed his arms. "Well, it worked."

Wolf tipped his head as if assessing him. "I think you should go home and I'll take care of Trill from here on out."

Not see Trill again? The anger drained out of him. He hadn't known her for two weeks yet, but couldn't imagine his life without her. Or the baby.

He hoped this wasn't another obsession. It was more intense then the feelings he'd had for Jamie. Pictures of Jamie consumed most of his early life, and when she started college, his father insisted he follow her there. Nearly his whole life, he'd been told she would be his wife.

That obsession paled next to the way his heart responded to Trill. He'd wanted to possess Jamie, but he would hand Trill his heart. Her needs were more important than his.

"Not happening. My premonition this morning saved both Trill and your grandmother. Art can easily find out Trill has a brother and come here looking for her." He flicked his gaze to Freesia. "Like he found her grandmother. She stands the best chance leaving with me." That might not be true. Art could have a tracking spell, but he wouldn't remind them.

Wolf glared. "You don't think your brother can put himself in your shoes and figure out where you go?"

"The only thing my brother knows about me is that I'm not a ruthless, power hungry killer like our father. That makes him think I'm weak."

Wolf shook his head. "I bet you can't even shoot. How are you going to protect my sister?"

Adam smirked. "Trill can shoot. Look, I had two premonitions that warned me to get Trill away. If you want, I can force a premonition every morning to see how the day will go."

Wolf's eyebrows rose. "You have premonitions on demand?"

Adam grinned. "Cool, huh?"

Wolf rolled his eyes. "Yeah, but, this morning, if Gram hadn't been there, how would you have saved my sister?"

Adam surveyed the two women then glared at Wolf. "This morning, I told them to get in the car and drive away, that I'd deal with Art. They refused." He bore his eyes into Trill. "I expect that if it's just the two of us, she'd leave if I told her to."

Wolf chuckled. "You don't know my sister." He crossed his arms. "You need a better plan."

Adam shrugged. He didn't know her that well yet, but he wanted to. "I can throw fireballs. The problem is they aren't as fast as bullets, so if my target sees it coming, he can get out of the way."

No sense mentioning being able to unlock locks without a key. No way was that a defensive skill. He gazed at Trill. "What about you? Art said you were powerful. What can you do?"

She shrugged. "I don't know about being powerful. You already know I can see a memory if someone allows it." His premonition she'd seen. "I can sense goodness or evil in people if I touch them. I can pick up on emotions, if they're strong enough. Those certainly aren't defensive, and didn't keep Art away from me."

Wolf cleared his throat. "There's more." His gaze darted to his grandmother and she gave a barely perceptible nod. He stared at Trill. "Mom died when Trill was eight. At the time, Trill thought she'd killed her."

Trill lurched forward. "What? Mom died of cancer, didn't she?"

Wolf nodded and stretched across the table, taking Trill's hands in his. "You blocked out her actual death, and Gram thought it was best to leave it that way." He glanced at his grandmother and back to Trill's scared face.

Adam didn't want to hear what Wolf was about to explain, and he could imagine that Trill wanted it even less. Wolf must have been ten or eleven at his mother's death.

Wolf sucked in a long breath and let it out slowly. "Mom was days from dying. We spent as much time with her as we could at hospice. On this particular day, silent tears ran down your face as soon as we stepped into the room. You climbed up on her bed, and put your little hands on her temples, and said, "Mommy hurts." It must have been really bad that day. Mom hugged you and said she was ready for you to take the pain away. I didn't know what she meant, and I don't think you did either." He glanced again at Freesia. "You closed your eyes and screwed your little face up like you were concentrating. After a couple of minutes, you smiled and said, *Mommy doesn't hurt anymore*. I noticed she wasn't breathing, and when you saw she'd died, you started screaming."

Trill's eyes widened and she tugged one hand away from her brother and covered her mouth. "I killed Mom?" She trembled, and tears spilled down her cheeks.

Adam scooted his chair closer and wrapped an arm around her shoulders. What a thing to find out.

Wolf stood, draped himself across the table, and took the hand back that she'd yanked away. "No, Trill. You gave Mom the peace she needed, so she could let go. The cancer is what took her."

Her shoulders relaxed. "What does that mean?"

"You can do more than read people's emotions, you can influence them."

"What? I can force people to be happy or sad?"

"Not force. You steer them towards memories that improve their mood. Of course, there's the flip side of that. If you were mean, you could steer them toward bad memories."

Her forehead creased. "How do you know how it works?"

"You told me. You even used it on me a few times when I was in a bad mood or mad at you." He grinned. "It was a gentle persuasion. You couldn't see the memory, but chose one that had the emotion you wanted me to have. I kind of wish you would have used it on me after Mom died and when Dad left, but you wouldn't do it anymore."

She shook her head. "I don't remember. How is this going to help with Art? I don't even know how to do it anymore."

"Maybe if Art found you," Wolf said, "you could pluck out one of his worst nightmares and use it to get away."

Adam squeezed her shoulder. "Try it on me. Make me happy."

He realized that he didn't need her influence to make him happy. He was, at least, content, with her in his presence. Once they got rid of the threat from Art, if she stayed with him, that would make him happy.

"Um. Okay." She cupped the side of his face with one hand, and squinted. Her gaze became unfocused, as if she searched inside him.

Adam closed his eyes as a memory rose up through a pool of dark water. His mother. Her smile always lifted his spirits, and it was so rare. He had her dark hair and blue eyes. He hoped he had a bit of her spirit, too. Ever since his sister had died of some lingering illness when she was three, his mom had spent several hours a couple days a week at the hospital. She visited deathly ill children whose families couldn't spend much time with them.

He'd had a day off school, and he'd begged to join her. He must have been about ten. She touched a finger to her lips. "We have to keep it a secret." It was one of the best days he'd had with his mother. Oh, some of it was difficult. Not all the children he played with would survive their illnesses, but he had a part in making them happy and helped them forget for a short time the reason they were in the hospital.

He blinked and stared into Trill's eyes. "Thank you."

She bit her lip. "You didn't look happy. I wasn't sure if I'd done it right."

He curled his fingers around the hand she still held to his face, and wrapped his other hand around it as well. "I remembered one of the happiest days I spent with my mother. She was relaxed and free and that made me happy. And it reminded me that I'm more like her than my father, and that makes me happy, too."

Wolf snorted. "So, your father is as bad as your brother?"

"He's worse."

Wolf leaped to his feet. "That's it. My sister's not going with you."

"And he's in prison." He didn't think four years was enough for kidnapping Jamie and trying to abort her baby, but at least the judge had also given him fifteen years for ordering the deaths of six men. Too bad they hadn't pinned that other death on him, the man he'd killed himself.

"Sit down," Freesia said with steel lacing her voice.

Wolf dropped like a stone onto his chair.

"Adam is a good man. He rescued Trillium when he didn't have to, and now he's invested in keeping the baby safe."

Wolf crossed his arms and glared at Adam. "Why is that? Because he's the baby's uncle? The kid's father doesn't feel that way."

Freesia curled her hands. "Because the baby's spirit bonded with Adam."

So that's what it was. For a fleeting second he wondered if the spirit had forced a connection, but it didn't matter. He cared. He probably already loved the baby. He'd seen the baby near death in two premonitions and didn't want it to happen in real life. And even more, he didn't want to see the knife plunge into Trill's chest again.

Adam let out a breath, trying to drive out tension. "I'll do everything in my power to keep them safe."

Chapter 7

Trill and Adam had been in the car for nearly five hours, driving to her uncle's hunting cabin in the Poconos. Twice she'd had to make them stop so she could use a restroom. Maybe she wouldn't have been embarrassed if she'd had a chance to gradually get used to the changes that pregnancy caused. Even when she was ten, she could make the trip without stopping. She would have had him stop again if they hadn't almost reached their destination.

Adam turned off the cleared, paved route onto a plowed, but still snow covered road edged with three foot banks of snow. Waves of yellow-brown sand coated the surface. Not surprising for the first of February.

"Is this it?" Adam asked, stopping beside a numbered post.

"Yes." Trill had never been to the cabin in winter, and it had been many years since her last visit. The best part of coming was swimming in the large pond behind the cabin. The water was so much warmer than the ocean near Gram's house. She'd be able to wander the pond now, if she could find it under the snow.

He took the turn. Uncle Elan had the driveway plowed. The house was out of sight behind a stand of evergreens.

Adam stopped in the cleared parking area in front of the cabin, got out and opened the trunk.

She couldn't take her eyes off the cabin. It hadn't changed, except to become a bit more weathered. The natural cedar shakes had aged to a steel gray. Some of the shingles on the roof had curled, indicating a summer project.

Four windows overlooked the drive, two together and two apart. A bump-out on the left was the bathroom addition. When she was young, there'd only been an outhouse. Then the summer she turned ten, Uncle Elan had built the bathroom, drilled a well, and installed a septic system. All the modern conveniences. Sort of.

Trill's door opened, and Adam stood beside it with her suitcase in his hand and his bag's strap over his shoulder. "Ready?"

"Yeah." She swung her legs out and he took her hand to help her stand. "Do you want me to grab some groceries?" They'd purchased them in the closest town.

"No. I'll come back out for them."

She led the way up the two steps and paused on the landing long enough to find her key and unlock the door. She was glad that whoever plowed had also shoveled.

It was dim inside, so she flipped the light switch, turning on a table lamp beside the door. The pine floors in all the rooms were painted a tan color, except the kitchen and bathroom, which were both covered in the same ugly olive green linoleum.

Adam stepped in beside her. "Where do you want these?"

"Back there." She pointed to the largest of the three bedrooms that lined the back of the living room. "I'll use this one. You can have your pick of the other two." The only queen bed would fit her and her belly. The other rooms had originally been one. Uncle Elan had divided it into two unequal sized rooms. The bigger one held two sets of bunk beds and the other was only big enough for one set and a three foot space beside it.

He dropped her suitcase on the bed and stuck his head into the other rooms, choosing the smaller one beside hers. "I'll go get the food now."

"Okay. I'll fire up the heat and turn on the water." Wolf had explained how to do it and told her if she forgot, there was a list of instructions taped on the inside of the closet door in the kitchen that held the appliances. She hoped it wouldn't take long to warm up. All the cabin had going for it at the moment was that it blocked the wind. And kept them hidden.

Hopefully, when they left here, they wouldn't be rushing away like at Gram's and would be able to do the shutdown procedure that was also in the instructions. First, she turned on the water and it rushed through the pipes. Then she turned on the gas, and lit the pilot lights for the water heater and furnace. A quick trip to the bathroom, and she returned to the kitchen as Adam closed kitchen cabinets. He opened the refrigerator and deposited their cold purchases onto the empty shelves, then opened the freezer with a pizza in his hand. "What's all this meat?"

She wandered up behind him. Each package was labeled with a letter. "V is for venison. PH is for pheasant. S is for squirrel. P—"

His eyes widened. "Squirrel? Seriously?"

She grinned. "Yeah. Some people say it tastes like chicken or pork. I think it's kind of gamey."

"I think I'll pass. So, what's this other stuff?"

"The P is porc…upine."

"Ser…"

She giggled. He probably thought she'd say pork. "R is for rabbit, which is actually pretty tasty."

He backed up, forcing her to retreat and closed the freezer. "It's a good thing we bought our own meat."

She glanced at the counter and squealed, picking up a

package of Fig Newtons. "I didn't see you buy these. Thank you." She tore the package open and took out two.

"I saw how much you liked them at your grandmother's."

Beside the fig bars sat the paperbacks she'd bought. Her uncle only had guys' reading material at the cabin. Books and magazines. Although Adam might not like hunting magazines, he'd probably enjoy some of the books. She might enjoy a couple of the spy novels.

Trill snatched up the books and dragged Adam to a four shelf bookcase in the corner of the living. "There are some books here."

He scanned the shelf and selected one. "Your uncle has Louis L'Amour books?" He raised his brows. "I can't believe a Native American would read westerns."

She grinned. "He's kind of open minded."

"I used to read these when I was a kid. I wonder if they still have appeal." He tossed the book onto the couch. "How long's it been since you were here?"

She frowned. "I think I was about sixteen. I would have probably kept coming if I had girl cousins that came, too. But it was Wolf and the boys."

He tipped his head toward the bedrooms. "Did your uncle make the separate room for you?"

"It was mostly for Gram and me. I feel bad about not coming anymore because Gram didn't get the chance to come anymore either. I don't know if she only came for me, or if she truly enjoyed it and gave it up for me."

He rested his hand on her shoulder, then strode to the couch, picked up the book and sat.

Trill dropped her books beside him and removed her coat. It wasn't quite warm enough yet, but she didn't want to struggle up off the couch in ten minutes to take it off. She hung it on a hook by the back door, and filled a glass with delicious water at the sink, better than any bottled water. She joined Adam on the couch.

He was already several pages into his book. "How old were you when your father left?"

Jeez. Where did that come from? A punch couldn't have been more painful. It had been such a traumatic time for all of them. She swallowed a lump. "Eight. It was the day after my mom's funeral."

He scooted next to her and wrapped his arm around her shoulders. "Oh, honey. I'm sorry I asked."

She stared at her feet. "H-he loved her so much, it tore him up. He signed the house over to Gram. She sold hers and moved in with us."

"How do you know that if you were only eight?"

"Gram told me when I was older." She didn't know which hurt worse, losing her mother to cancer or her father to grief. They'd been such a happy family six months before that.

He took her hand. "Have you seen him since?"

She shook her head. "I don't even know if he's alive."

"My mother died in a car accident when I was sixteen. A teenager goofing off with his friends ran a red light and t-boned us. I just got a bump on my head, but I watched Mom die before help arrived. She…told me she loved me, then passed out. The paramedics arrived and said she…was dead."

Trill squeezed Adam's hand. They'd both watched their mothers die. She had a feeling it had changed his life as much as it had hers.

"Dad sued the driver's family. Got a ton of money. I didn't care. I just wanted Mom back."

She tipped her head onto his shoulder. She already knew his mother was important to him because of the happy memory she'd found. At least, she'd had Gram and Wolf after she lost her parents. They were the reason she had made it through the pain of her loss. Adam had nobody.

"Was your dad a good father before your mom died?"

He tensed. "He was always a bastard. Mom just tempered it a bit. Art's always said Dad loved me more than him. I don't buy it. I don't think he's ever loved either of us."

That must have been hard to accept. Even though her dad left, he still loved them. He'd just loved their mother more. "Why did Art think that?"

He huffed out a breath. "Sometimes I intentionally screwed up something Dad wanted me to do because I didn't think it was right. He'd say I took after my mother. Oh, I'd get punished, but not as bad as Art would when he tried his hardest to do what Dad expected, and it didn't turn out."

She was afraid to ask, but wanted to know Adam. "What kind of punishment did you get?" She was sure it was worse than being sent to his room or denied privileges, like she'd had.

"Dad would stare."

She frowned. That didn't seem so bad. "Stare?"

He sucked in a breath. "And then the pain would start. Sometimes it felt like my back was burning from a whip striking it, or sometimes it felt like my fingers were breaking, one at a time."

She palmed the side of his neck and pressed her forehead into his shoulder. "Oh. My. God."

"The pain would last for a few seconds or a few minutes, and then it was gone, like nothing happened. Art usually suffered longer or more intensely. You can't cry child abuse if there's no evidence."

She rested her cheek on his chest. "What about your mom?"

"Mom didn't know about it because we always had these discussions in Dad's study, and he said it would be worse if we told her."

Any decent mother would have run with her children to protect them from her husband if she'd found out, but a young boy wouldn't think of that. Maybe his evil father would have found and hurt his mother for the betrayal. Then that boy would have no one to show him love.

Trill couldn't imagine silently suffering through what Adam had. And he'd survived it with a kind spirit, but his brother let it turn him into a monster.

Trill rubbed her fingers on his neck. "I wish someone could have helped you."

He shrugged. "What's done is done. I am who I am because of it." He pulled her hand from his neck and kissed the fingertips. "Okay. Childhood confessions over. How about we put together something for dinner?"

Whoa. That light touch packed more of a punch than it had any right to. She couldn't imagine the feeling a real kiss from Adam would provoke. She forced the thought away. It wasn't worth thinking about since she was so far from her best. And soon she'd be a pregnant whale.

***

Adam sat at the kitchen table, coffee cup in hand, and his laptop in front of him. He'd kept it in his car trunk the entire time they'd been at Freesia's.

He'd peeked in at Trill before showering. She'd been sleeping on her side, one pillow under her head and one clenched in her arms. He so much wished he was that pillow. Either of them. Both of them. Her head on his shoulder and their arms around each other.

He ran a hand through his still damp hair, and blew out a long breath. This was so not an obsession, at least, not the same kind. With Jamie, his only thought was to make her his. He hadn't tried to force her, but he'd bided his time and did his best to make her want him, with no thought as to what would happen next if he got her. With Trill, he definitely wanted her, but his imagination planned a whole life with her. Raising this child, having more children, and doing whatever was necessary to make her happy. He wanted the whole package that was Trill.

He rubbed his eyes. He needed to concentrate on keeping Trill safe, and part of that was figuring out how to end the baby's usefulness to Art.

He turned on the hotspot for his phone and checked his email messages. Nothing important…except the last one. From Art.

> *I was surprised to see you this morning, brother. How dare you take her for yourself. I've got the ritual and you've got the girl. I suggest we work together and both benefit from the increase in power. Since we are both blood to my baby, we can both gain nearly as much power as one of us alone.*
>
> *If you don't call me, she's all mine when I find her. And I* <u>*will*</u> *find her again.*
>
> *Art*

Adam couldn't believe Art thought he'd kidnapped Trill to do the ritual himself. Art saw Adam through his own twisted needs.

Now, he was sure Art hadn't found Trill through her grandmother, but because he tracked her somehow. And he needed to find out how, so he could block it as extra protection, in case the medicine bag Freesia had made didn't work.

He wished he had access to his dad's library. Adam didn't have a single book on abilities, or witchcraft—he shuddered—in his own home, even if he'd been home to check it out. The few books his grandparents had kept at the house, he'd given to his father. At the time, he didn't feel he'd have a need for more knowledge on spells or power. He had what he had, and that was good enough for him. Apparently, not anymore.

He'd stew on it a bit, and maybe something would come to him. He disconnected the laptop from his phone's hotspot, and got up to make breakfast.

***

Trill woke to the wonderful aroma of bacon and coffee. She stretched and grimaced. The doctor had told her to limit her caffeine intake, and they hadn't bought decaf. Maybe she'd have a half cup, and some orange juice.

She threw on her robe and headed for the bathroom. Since breakfast seemed ready, she'd have her shower after eating. She used the toilet, brushed her teeth, and ran a brush through her hair. Semi-presentable. At least, the dark circles under her eyes had disappeared after being at Gram's. She closed her eyes and drew in a long breath. Like that was going to make her more attractive with this big belly.

She ran her hands over her stomach. "Sorry, baby. I'm not used to you yet or used to thinking like a mother."

She headed to the kitchen, and found Adam at the stove, stirring eggs in a pan. "Good morning. That smells wonderful."

He smiled over his shoulder, and her stomach made a little flip. He was so attractive. His rumpled hair indicated he'd run his hands through it. That was something she wanted to do. Those pale eyes seemed to laser into her.

He nodded toward the coffee machine. "Coffee's ready."

She poured herself a half cup and topped off his.

"Thanks. You're only having a half cup?"

She shrugged. "The doctor said I should limit caffeine."

His mouth dropped open. “I forgot. I should have gotten decaf.”

“That’s all right. I forgot, too.” She poured a glass of orange juice.

He dished up the eggs and added bacon to their plates, then carried them to the table. She followed with her drinks, then returned for his coffee.

She set his cup down and her sleeve brushed the mouse pad on his open laptop and woke it up. Art’s name caught her attention. She read through the email.

No! It couldn’t be. Did he bring her out here so she’d be isolated? Did he already email Art the cabin’s address and was waiting like nothing had changed until his brother arrived?

Her insides froze. He was like his brother, only more devious. She wanted to make him feel her cold pain. “You contacted your brother?”

His eyes widened at the laptop screen and his gaze darted to her. “No. I read his email. I’m not going to respond. You know I don’t want him to find you.”

He sounded sincere, and she didn’t feel like he manipulated her thoughts the way Art had. As if she even remembered how that felt. “Do I?”

“Trill, please.”

She wanted to believe him. It didn’t mean she should. She wanted him to feel cold inside. She’d steal his keys and leave. Go anywhere but here. He could tell his brother she’d slipped away after she was gone.

***

She glared at Adam and slammed her palm into his chest, her focus too intense. “Trill, listen. Please.” Cold spread through his chest. It crept across his shoulders and down his arms, then slid past his waist and into his legs. First it froze the surface, and then it penetrated deeper and deeper. "What are you doing?"

Tears streaked down her cheeks. "You want to join your brother to kill the baby and me."

"No!" He tried to reach out to her, but his arm was a popsicle at his side. "I'm doing everything I can to keep Art away from you because I don't want you to die. I'm not doing it for leverage. I'm falling in love with you."

She stood a foot from him, her arm stretched out, her lip caught between her teeth.

He understood her fear. She hadn't had two weeks yet to deal with what had happened to her. "Look. If I'd wanted leverage, I could have stuck around your apartment until Art showed up. Or at your grandmother's, I wouldn't have told you about the premonition. You would have been trapped in the house when he got there."

Her hands clenched together, but the frigid numbness remained.

She dropped her hands to her sides and leaned forward. "We almost didn't get away."

"But I gave you my keys and told you to leave. You and your gram would have gotten away."

"You could have jumped into Art's car with him and followed us."

He tipped his head back and tried to haul in a deep breath. The iciness in his lungs constricted them, allowing only shallow breaths. He stared into her anguished face. "I had nothing to do with what Art wrote. Check the message. I didn't reply to him. He doesn't understand what it means to care for someone. He only craves power and doesn't care who he has to hurt to get it. That's not me. He doesn't understand me. I thought you did."

Trill stared into his eyes for almost a minute. "Oh,

Adam." She wrapped her arms around his frozen body. "I don't know how to reverse this. I've never done it before. I didn't know I could."

He wished he could wrap his popsicles around her. It was the first time she'd hugged him and he couldn't feel it. His mind raced. "What did you feel when you froze me?"

"It was like a cold rage. And I directed it at you."

Since, she'd plucked out a happy memory for him, maybe that would help her, too. "Think of a time when you were on a beach, the sun beating down on you. Sometime you were having fun there with Wolf or a friend."

Her hair tickled his chin, but he couldn't feel her rubbing the side of her head against his chest. "Okay."

He hoped this worked. If she didn't thaw him, his extremities and then his organs would get frostbite. He'd die of exposure inside a heated cabin. "Once you feel nice and warm, force that warmth into me the same way you did the cold."

Seconds ticked by. Nothing happened. It hadn't worked. Then a painful warmth penetrated his chest. He dragged in a lungful of air and his insides prickled as if hot needles dive bombed him. He'd never complain again about the pins and needles of warming toes and fingers.

Her arms, warm around him, and her baby bump pressed against…not going there. Too late. Warm blood rushed to that appendage, shooting it full of spikes. He couldn't hold in the grunt of pain.

Trill's arms tightened around him. "I'm hurting you."

His arms were finally freed from their icy imprisonment and he enclosed her in them. "No, that was me. All me." He would never tell her how much pain freezing and thawing had given him. It would cause her pain to know that.

She dropped her arms and tugged, but he didn't let her go.

"Trill?"

She tipped her face up, and he kissed her. He wasn't sure how she'd respond. Although, he'd convinced her that he wouldn't harm her, he was still the brother of the man who wanted to kill her and the baby.

She slid her hands up his ribs, over his chest and around his neck. Her lips opened for him and he deepened the kiss. She tasted like a summer day at the ocean and a hint of toothpaste. Her lips were softer and more giving than he expected. He'd take everything he could get. His body swung from frozen to overheated in a few minutes. Trill still didn't fully trust him, so he drew back, dropped a kiss on her nose, and smiled at her.

Her eyes twinkled. "So, you forgive me?"

He chuckled. "There's nothing to forgive. You panicked. I understand what you've been through."

She dropped her head onto his shoulder. "I wish I did."

Chapter 8

Trill trudged behind Adam. She was beginning to think she shouldn't have suggested a walk in the woods, but she'd gone stir crazy after being stuck inside for three days. And she had meant a walk and not a hike, but that was what it had turned into because when the trail forked a couple of times, she couldn't remember which way they should take to keep it short.

They'd had to break a fresh path through six inches of snow to get to the main trail.

Sometimes they could trek side-by-side, but when the path narrowed, every few minutes, Adam checked back to make sure she followed. There. A perfect rock beside the trail someone had already cleared of snow.

"Adam, I'm taking a break." She dropped onto it without waiting for a response, and uncapped the bottle of water resting in a sling across her shoulder. She gulped down a few swallows, then sucked in long breaths and blew them out, almost feeling her oxygen starved body absorb it. She hadn't expected to be this out of shape, but she probably hadn't gotten much exercise over the past few months. And then there was the baby belly. It was wonderful to get out, though.

She glanced down the path. Adam had disappeared. Maybe he hadn't heard her tell him she was stopping. As soon as he returned, she'd tell him she was ready to head back to the cabin.

She wrenched her gaze back the way they'd come when heavy feet trudged the path. An athletic man marched up the trail, a hiking stick in one hand matching his steps. Dark hair that nearly touched his shoulders peeked out from a blue wool cap.

He stopped beside her, and her stomach clenched. "Hi, there. Are you all right?"

People always seemed to be concerned for pregnant women and she hoped this was no different. She glanced up the path. Still no Adam. "I'm with someone, but he apparently got ahead of me. I'm sure he'll be back any minute."

The man pointed over his shoulder. "I didn't pass anyone."

She nodded in the direction they'd been heading. "He's up there somewhere."

"Do you want me to wait with you or walk with you?"

She'd never been asked that before when she hiked alone. She felt at a disadvantage, seated and pregnant. And he had bulging muscles and a hiking stick.

"Um, okay. I guess I've rested long enough." She could have used a few more minutes, but now she was uncomfortable sitting alone with a stranger towering over her. She didn't want to tell him to continue on, and have him refuse. Then the ruse would be up, if there was one.

He took her hand as she started to rise. She wished neither of them wore gloves, so she could sense his spirit. She tugged her hand away once she was on her feet. He was a half head taller than her. "Thanks."

"I'm Jeff." He gave her a dazzling smile, as if she wasn't nearly six months pregnant.

"Trill."

"That's an unusual name."

"So I've been told." This portion of the trail was wide enough for two and he fell in beside her. His hiking stick shushed rhythmically as he stabbed it into the snow. She was sort of surprised he hadn't offered it to her to use.

"It's unique, like you."

This man didn't know her, and wouldn't know if she was unique. Unease squirmed inside her, and she wished she had a way to touch him skin-to-skin. Something about him and the situation didn't feel right.

She purposely caught her toe on a rock sticking above the snow and stumbled, catching herself with her palm on a tree. She slid her hand down, out of her glove, scraping her palm across the bark. "Ow!"

Jeff grabbed her arm. "Are you all right?"

"I may have gotten a sliver."

He took his gloves off and stuffed them in his pockets. "Here. Let me see."

She held her hand out, little bits of bark stuck to it. It felt a bit raw, but she didn't think anything had imbedded.

He took her hand in one of his and slid the other from her fingertips to palm. He studied her palm and repeated on one spot. "There. It's just a bit scraped." He retrieved her glove from the ground and slipped it onto her hand.

His actions seemed to show he was kind, but she'd sensed no emotion from his touch. Consciously or unconsciously, he'd been blocking. Fear slammed into her. Art must have found her and sent this man to deliver her to him, and he faked concern to fool her or turn her over to Art unharmed. Maybe Jeff had an accomplice who had already done something to Adam.

She'd gotten them into this mess. It had been her idea to trek into the woods. Now they were a couple of miles from the cabin and Adam's car. He'd promised to force a premonition every morning. Why hadn't he seen this?

She could freeze this guy, but she didn't have enough evidence to not trust him. Maybe he had a natural skill to block his mind. She needed to find Adam in case this guy had a friend who had taken him. Her best option was to pretend nothing was wrong. "Do you hike out here much?"

"It's the first time on this trail for me. What about you?"

"It's been years since I've been out here." She wished she could turn around and head back, but not without Adam. He should have returned to her by now.

She rubbed over the medicine bag, reassured it was still under her coat. She'd only taken the bag off to shower. Art shouldn't have been able to find her.

The hiking stick stabbed harder in the snow. "What do you think of it?"

Too many thoughts had run through her head to follow the question. Oh, yeah. The trail. "I wish we'd gone the other way. I forgot how hilly this trail is, and harder…in my condition." As if he wouldn't have noticed she was pregnant.

"We aren't far from the parking lot. You'll make it. No problem."

"Except we're not parked there." The moment she said it, she wished she hadn't. It would have been better to let him think their car was parked nearby. At least, there were other trailheads where a car could be parked. He might not guess they were in a cabin, but she wouldn't feel safe there any longer anyway.

"Oh. I can drive you to your car."

No frickin' way. She didn't know what would happen when they arrived at the parking lot, but she wouldn't get in a car with a guy she couldn't read.

"Thanks, but I think my friend will be waiting there." He would have come back for her, but she couldn't let on that she was concerned.

They rounded a bend and there was the parking lot.

Jeff grabbed her arm. "Careful of the hole there."

It wasn't any worse than some of the others they'd passed, but he didn't let go of her arm once they'd cleared it. His grip tightened when she tried to yank away.

Two cars were parked in the lot, with a man standing beside the closest one. As they rounded the car, she gasped at the sight of Adam sitting on the ground with his hands tied behind his back. He glared at the man grasping his shoulder.

"Sorry, Trill." His defeated expression tore at her, but she wouldn't give up. Too much was at stake.

She tugged her arm, but the man only squeezed harder. She tried to keep the panic from her voice. "What's going on here?"

"You have an appointment with the father of your baby," the closer man said.

Art must have given these men some sob story about her leaving him for another man and he wouldn't get to see his child.

She spun, tugged off the glove on her free hand with her teeth, and slapped her palm on the man's chest. She sent cold into his body. It might take longer to penetrate through his coat. She tried to make it more frigid, just in case. She hoped the other man didn't realize what she was doing before it was his turn.

The man's eyes widened. "What are you doing to me?"

She yanked her arm out of his hand. "I figure it takes a cold man to turn a pregnant woman over to an abuser, so I'm just making you feel what you are."

Something clunked against the car behind her and she glanced over her shoulder. The other man was crumpled on the ground with Adam sitting on his chest.

"What did you do to him?" Trill asked.

Adam lifted one shoulder. "I rolled into him then kicked him in the head." He leaned forward, awkwardly getting to his feet, and turned his back to her. "Would you mind cutting me loose?"

She inspected the living statue in front of her, figuring she was safe to turn her back on him. The zip-ties had cut deep into the skin of Adam's poor wrists. "I don't have a knife."

"I've got a small one in my right, front pocket."

Okay, she could do this. Hopefully, there wasn't a lot in his pocket and the knife would be easy to find. Not like scrabbling around in the bottom of her purse, chasing down an errant key.

She slipped her hand into his pocket, and glanced up at him when he sucked in a breath. Okay. It affected him, too. She fished out his keys to clear the way, and dove back in. Her fingers touched metal. Yes. She wrapped her hand around it and withdrew it. She opened the blade and carefully started sawing on the zip-tie, not wanting to tug on it.

"Faster, Trill."

"I don't want to hurt you."

"Just do it."

She pushed harder as she sawed and he whipped his hands apart. He rubbed one wrist and then the other. They were dented and red.

She glanced between the two strangers. "What about them?"

He pulled zip-ties from the unconscious man's pocket. "I'll tie them up, then we'll load them into their car. We'll drive it back to the cabin, and load our stuff into my car. Then we'll drive both cars to that grocery store we stopped at and leave the guys and their car there."

By the time Adam finished talking, both men's hands were tied behind their backs, and he had both their keys. He wrestled the first man into the backseat of the car and shoved him all the way across. The second man took longer since he was stiff as an icicle. Adam ended up tipping the guy from a distance away and sliding him in like a log, then tied their ankles.

He crossed his arms and stared at the men. “How long will it take your guy to thaw out?”

She jerked her palms up. “How am I supposed to know? I’ve only done it to you, and I melted you. I’m sure if it was summer it would be pretty fast, but with as cold as it is, maybe he won’t thaw until his friend turns on the heat.”

At this point, she didn’t care if it took all night.

The second car key Adam tried worked. “You drive so I can watch these guys.”

She pulled onto the main road and turned right. “How’d the guy get you?”

He touched her arm. “I’m sorry. I had things on my mind and forgot to make sure you were right behind me. I hadn’t gone far when this guy passed me, and we said hello. Then I remembered you and turned, but he hit me on the side of the head with his hiking stick, and then punched me in the gut. I dropped, and he jumped on my back and zip-tied my hands, then marched me to the car. None of this would have happened if I’d stayed near you and paid attention.”

“They still would have tried to get us.”

“But we would have been together.”

She glanced in the rearview mirror at the unconscious men. “Now, what are we going to do?”

“Let’s not talk about it until we’ve dumped these two. They might be faking.”

“I think we should dump them first since we have to winterize the cabin before we leave.” That would take about a half-hour, and she didn’t want the men waking up in the car while they were still at the cabin.

“Can’t we just leave it?”

“Adam, it’s January. I’m not leaving Uncle Elan’s cabin

to get frozen pipes when he so graciously loaned it to us."

He huffed out a breath. "Fine. We'll pick up my car and drop this one off at that store, then return to the cabin. We're going to lose an hour in travel time alone."

"Where are—"

He stuck up his index finger. "Shh. Not in front of the children."

***

Between picking up his car to drop the other one at the store, and winterizing the cabin and packing, they'd lost two-and-a-half hours that could have gotten them far away from their attackers. At least, he'd had the chance to get more money at the bank across from the grocery store since Art would already know where they were.

Adam drew in a slow breath, and breathed out through his mouth, trying to blow out the tension. He flexed his fingers over the steering wheel. They were fine. Now, to disappear.

Trill twisted towards him, slipping one leg up on the car seat. "How did they find us this time? I'm pretty sure I wouldn't have talked about my uncle's cabin with Art."

He rubbed the back of his neck and tried to massage out some tightness. "I think it might have been me. He likely can't track you since you have the medicine bag, but now he knows I'm with you."

She dug into her purse. "I have an idea. Let me call Gram." She called up the number and waited. "Gram." She fidgeted with the hem of her shirt. "Art found us, so we're on the road." She glanced at him. "No, it wasn't too bad." She shifted in her seat. "We think that maybe Art tracked Adam this time." She nodded. "Yeah. That's what I was wondering. Do you think there's enough in my medicine bag to split it between us?" She retrieved a pen and paper from her purse. "All right, I'm ready." She scribbled on the paper, then stuffed it into her purse. "Thanks, Gram. Wish me luck." She dropped the phone into her purse.

He flicked his gaze to her. "You're splitting your medicine bag between us?"

"Yes. Gram gave me a spell to strengthen its power."

His hold on the steering wheel tightened. "Do you think it will work for both of us? The bag was only meant to protect you." If he'd thought about it at Wolf's place, he would have had Freesia make him a bag, too. Now, they didn't have that option. Maybe he should take her somewhere safe and leave her with the whole medicine bag. He glanced at her. He couldn't leave her. Art was too desperate to not come up with a different way to find her, and she'd be alone. He couldn't do it. They would stay together for the duration.

"Gram thinks so."

At least, it could buy them some time, get her further along. If Art got his hands on her, the baby would have a greater chance of surviving. But Trill…No. Art wasn't going to get her.

She crossed her arms above her belly. "How come you didn't see these guys today in a premonition?"

"I concentrated on Art. He was in his home office, on his computer, on his phone. I didn't think anything of it. I just thought he was far away from us, so we had nothing to worry about." He glanced at her. "From now on, I'm making you the center of my premonition. I'm pretty sure I would have seen those guys if I'd done that."

"What about you? Why don't you put yourself in your premonition?"

He shook his head. "If I concentrate on me, it's fuzzy and incomplete. I don't get useful information. The last premonition, I was in it unconscious on the floor. But I wasn't the focus. At the time, I thought Art was, but it could have been you. Anyway, when we get to a motel, I'll try a premonition centered on you."

"Okay."

He captured her hand. He liked her warm touch, and it gave him a rush of pleasure. "We should name the baby. Um. You should." He loved this baby, but was afraid to claim him. First he'd have to claim Trill, and he didn't know if she'd ever be ready for that, knowing who his brother was.

Her eyebrows spiked. "We should?"

"Do you want to keep referring to him as 'the baby' and 'he'? We know he's a boy, so why not?"

She rubbed her tummy. "You're right. Let's name him."

His heart lightened when she included him. "Do you want to give him a Wampanoag name? You can't name him after a flower. No appropriate animals pop into my head."

She giggled. "I couldn't bring myself to call my baby Badger or Bear. I think Wolf got the best animal name, and I'm not naming the baby after his uncle."

For a second, he thought she meant him, but realized she meant Wolf. "What's your father's name?" At her torn expression, he wished he hadn't asked.

"Jonathan. But I'm not naming him after a man who couldn't stick around and be a father."

He wanted to brighten her mood again. "An ordinary Jonathan? I thought it might be Cloud or Oak or Storm."

She grinned. "Nope. Just ordinary." She bit her lipped and stared at him. "I've always liked Lucas."

"Luke, huh?"

"No. Lucas."

He tipped his head. "You know a lot of people will call him Luke."

She shrugged. "When he's old enough, he can choose how he introduces himself."

"That's it? Two minutes and you've got a name? Some people take months and they still don't have a name when the baby's born."

"You think it's all right, don't you?"

"I think it's perfect. Lucas Song or Luke Song. Both sound good to me." Maybe even Lucas Richards, except that would be giving the baby the same last name as the man who wanted him and his mother dead.

He rubbed Trill's belly. "What do you think little one? Do you like Lucas?"

She gasped, and bracketed her belly with her hands. "I think he just did a somersault. I don't know if that means he liked it or not."

It thrilled him to feel the little guy move. "I think he liked it. What kind of vibes do you get?"

She closed her eyes, and a smile touched her lips. "I think he likes it."

"Wouldn't it be great if all babies could be asked if they liked their names? There would probably be fewer Biffs, Dicks, and Barts."

She laughed. "Okay. I've met a Dick or two. Ohmygod. But never a Biff or Bart."

"See. Maybe these babies do talk to their parents."

She seemed more relaxed, finally. "Where are we headed?"

He shrugged. "I don't know. I figured we'd head north a while and then find some little town a few miles off the highway."

"Okay."

She was so trusting. She could have stayed at her brother's, but she'd chosen to join him. He'd insisted on her coming with him, but the others could have vetoed him and there would have been nothing he could do. Now, he was the only one responsible for keeping Trill safe, and that was one job he didn't intend to fail at—although, he'd sure come close more than once.

She extracted her medicine bag from under her shirt. "I think we should stop soon and make your medicine bag."

"What are we going to put mine in?"

"I've got a sachet in my suitcase I can empty out."

"Do I need it around my neck, like you? Or can I put it in my pocket?"

"Your pocket's fine for now, but we should put a string on it, so you can wear it while you sleep."

"Let's do it when we stop for dinner." He hoped the divided bag would be strong enough for both of them. There was no way to test it.

Chapter 9

Adam had taken a random exit, and drove a while before turning into an independent motel. It was remote enough to be safe for the night. Neither of them would be able to tolerate the close quarters of a motel room for more than a few days.

He entered the office alone. An old monitor and keyboard sat on the worn counter. Numbered cubby-holes were within arms reach of the workstation. Sitting at the end of the counter, a small rack held sightseeing brochures.

A white-haired man with wire-framed glasses sat at a desk behind the counter, and glanced up from writing on a legal pad. “Evening, young man. Would you like a room?”

Adam rested his forearms on the desk. “Yes, I’d like a room with two beds farthest from the road.”

The man tapped a paper encased in a protective sleeve with diagrams of the rooms, most with dates on them. “You can have a double or be far from the road, not both.” He tapped a square beside the one marked ‘office’. “This is a double.” He tapped another square, second to last in the row. “This is the farthest from the road that’s available, but it’s a single.”

Adam stared out the window. They weren’t on a major highway, but he’d hoped to hide his car at the end of the building, around the corner. He also wanted their room close enough to the car in case they needed to make a fast getaway. "All right. I'll take this one." He tapped the farthest room. He settled up and the man grabbed a key from a cubby.

He hoped Trill didn't mind sharing. He could do this. He had a month of practice, sleeping beside Jamie. He hadn't tried to make love to her, although he'd wanted to. Of course, she'd always kept a pillow between them. Trill didn't have a boyfriend back home keeping them apart. Just his brother who wanted to kill her.

It didn't hurt as much as it used to that Jamie had rejected him. He hadn't pressured her, but he'd tried to make her see that she needed him. While she was in college, he'd gotten her to go on a couple dates with him, and talked to her every chance he got, but even the month they'd been imprisoned together wasn't enough to sway her to see him as anything but a friend. Maybe not even that.

Now, he was ecstatic nothing had come of it. The love he had for Trill, in the short time he'd known her, was more than the pale version of love he'd had for Jamie. If anything, his feelings for Jamie had been infatuation. Without realizing it, he'd forced himself to care for her because he was supposed to.

He drove the car behind the building. "We're in room twenty-three."

They got out and he grabbed their bags from the trunk. She telescoped the handle on her bag and followed him into the room.

She stopped in the doorway, her gaze on the bed. "There's only one bed." She glared at him.

"The other room was too close to the road. I thought this was the safer option." He raised his hands in the air, spreading his fingers. "Strictly hands off." Either she trusted him or she didn't.

She grabbed night clothes and toothbrush from her

suitcase, and disappeared into the bathroom.

The room wasn't half bad. The small, round table and two chairs near the window were fairly new. The bed didn't sag in the middle, so Trill wouldn't end up rolling into him, which he would love, but she probably wouldn't.

The TV wasn't large, but it was a flat screen. He turned it on and flipped through channels until he found a comedy he thought Trill might like.

After Trill returned in a knee length nightgown and climbed into bed, he took his turn in the bathroom. It gave him a jolt seeing her in his bed. Yeah, he'd watched her climb in, but there she sat, blankets up over her tummy, and he got to climb in beside her. He'd promised to keep his hands off her, and he would, even though every fiber and nerve in him wanted to fold her into his arms.

***

Trill opened her eyes. Daylight peaked between the drapes. Her head rested on Adam's bare shoulder and his arm circled her back, with his hand on her hip. Her tummy pressed against his side and her knee touched his thigh. And they were on his side of the bed, so he'd kept his promise, at least, until she scooted into his space.

The night before had been tense, sitting side-by-side, but not close enough to touch, as they watched TV for an hour or so. She'd been too nervous to converse, so they hadn't talked much. She'd given up and decided it was time to get some sleep.

Now, she cuddled into him and wished she could wake every morning like this.

His voice rumbled under her cheek. "I like this."

She jerked her head up.

He smiled, then kissed her nose. "Good morning."

She dug her elbow into the mattress, but he stopped her.

"No. Stay a bit longer."

Trill lowered her head back to Adam's chest and relaxed. He seemed to like this close contact as much as she did. And he didn't try anything else.

He rubbed his hand on her hip, sending pleasant shivers through her. Just the smallest almost intimate touch made her want him, but she was half a whale, working her way to full whale status. Who would want this if the baby wasn't even his?

His other hand rubbed her belly. That was in the forefront of his head all the time, keeping her baby safe. Although she wished she was as important, this wasn't about her.

I little foot kicked out, hitting his target.

Adam chuckled. "I think Lucas is practicing soccer."

She loved the sound of that. She hadn't talked to the baby using his name yet. It was nice that Adam was the first to use it.

He kissed the top of her head. "We better get going." It sounded like a bit of reluctance in his voice.

"Okay." This time, she did push up. Now to get all the way to the far edge of the bed. Adam must have noticed her dilemma because he sat up and swung them both around, so their feet touched the floor.

He kissed her temple. They'd crossed some line in the last twenty-four hours. She liked it.

He stood and helped her to her feet. "You go shower, and I'll search for somewhere we can stay."

***

Two hours to their destination should have been a breeze. The day before, Trill had been able to last longer before needing a bathroom stop. A little longer might be possible. She didn't want to ask Adam to stop or how long until they got there, like a little kid. He wouldn't tell her where they were going or what their accommodations were.

"Ten minutes until we're there. You holding up okay?"

"I'm fine as long as it's only ten minutes, and I get to use a bathroom at the office."

He glanced at her. "They might as well meet you, since we should be there a while. On the phone, I told them I was bringing my wife. Only one last name to give out. I hope that's all right with you." His gaze remained on her longer this time.

Her heart leaped. If only. "That's fine."

The turn signal clicked on, and he turned into a driveway, and passed over a bridge with a bubbling brook beneath.

"An RV park? I figured you'd found cabins."

"This place does have cabins, but they've got a couple travel trailers, too. I thought it might be more comfortable than a rustic cabin."

"Don't they have small bathrooms? I'm kind of taking up the space of two right now."

He shrugged. "I don't know. I've never been in one. We'll ask if they have one with a bigger bathroom."

He stopped in front of a small trailer with an office sign and got out. She joined him in front of the car and he took her hand. She'd have to keep it hidden since she didn't have a ring. Maybe it didn't even matter.

As soon as they entered the office, Trill headed towards a door marked *Restroom*. The outside door opened again and a woman bustled in.

"You must be Adam Chandler. I'm Beth Sawyer."

Trill hadn't known he'd used a fake last name on the phone, but it made sense.

"Yes."

In the restroom, Trill could hear their voices, but not what was said. She joined Adam at the counter, and he wrapped an arm around her waist.

Beth slid a printed sheet toward him. "Here, sign this. I'll leave that unit open in case you do stay longer. By the way, what made you decide to come out here in the dead of winter? Your wife won't be up for hunting or snow shoeing."

Trill startled, not sure how to answer the question, and Adam held her closer. Hearing someone refer to her as Adam's wife, sent a pleasant tingle through her.

He rubbed her belly. "Teri's grandmother gave us a stack of money and said we better get our postponed honeymoon in before the baby came. I wasn't about to pass that gift up."

Great way to explain away handing over a fistful of cash. She didn't know if she should be worried that Adam told a lie so well. And now she had to remember her name was Teri.

"I'm surprised you didn't go someplace warm."

Adam rubbed her belly again. "We didn't want to risk the pregnancy by flying." He smirked. "And it would have taken forever to drive anywhere warm with a bathroom break every couple of hours."

Beth chuckled. "Oh, I remember those days."

Trill liked Adam's hands on her, even if it was a lie for Beth.

Adam signed and Beth dropped a key on the counter, then pointed out the door. "Take the second left and you'll find your RV near the end. Numbered posts are in front of every spot."

He snatched up the key. "Thanks." They spun around and hurried out the door.

Trill tugged on her arm, but he wouldn't let her go. "You told her my name is Teri."

"Your name is too unique while we're hiding.

Otherwise, I think Trill is a perfect name for you."

Adam followed Beth's directions. About half of the pad spaces were empty. She wondered how many of the RVs scattered about were owned by the park. Adam found their trailer, and parked beside the attached deck. The trailer wasn't as large as most of the others, but she wouldn't want to haul it around.

He lifted her suitcase out of the trunk and set it on the ground. She extended the handle, grabbed a bag of groceries, and took the two steps onto the deck and stopped at the RV door. Adam followed with the rest of the bags. He set some on the wood floor and juggled to insert the key in the lock, then shouldered the door open.

Trill stepped into a little kitchen, set her grocery bag on the counter and continued inside to give Adam room to get into the small space. Not all of his bags fit on the counter, so he set some of them on the floor.

Trill took a slow spin. "This is really nice. It's not as big as my uncle's cabin, but it beats that motel room by a lot. I couldn't imagine hiding out there longer than a night."

A dining table and benches sat in a slide-out alcove with enough space to seat four. She released her roller bag and took a few steps into the living room area. A cushy couch took up most of two walls, across from a fireplace with a large screen TV above it. A fake bearskin rug covered the carpet in front of the small hearth.

"I can't believe there's a fireplace in here."

Adam came up behind her, and lightly rested a hand on her hip. "It must run on propane." He chuckled. "This has to be the honeymoon RV."

The comfortable sized living room took up the entire end of the trailer. She retraced her steps, and wandered through an open door. On her left, was a bathroom she could deal with. The shower was large enough to accommodate her if she was nine months pregnant. Continuing into the room, she found a queen-size bed and a built in dresser. A door beside the dresser must be the closet. A TV hung on the wall shared by the bathroom. A perfect little room with just enough space to walk on three sides of the bed.

One bed. In the entire RV. They'd shared a bed last night, they could do it again. Except she'd probably make a fool of herself. When they'd woke that morning, she'd been an invader on Adam's side of the bed.

***

Adam and Trill sat next to each other on the couch. He'd been surprised when she plopped down within a foot of him. He'd taken the prime TV viewing spot, but she still could have sat half a room from him. He liked that she chose to sit so close.

He'd found a rerun of a crime show that he enjoyed, but hadn't seen in a while.

She sat cross-legged and, propped one knee on his thigh. "I love CSI."

He liked that she touched him, even if accidentally. Before long, she scooted closer, so their arms touched, and tipped her head against his shoulder. It reminded him of being a teen boy and incrementally getting closer and closer to a girl. Two could play this game. He took her hand and rested them atop her thigh. He wished it was summer and she wore shorts, so he could feel more of her skin.

He jumped as sirens on TV yanked his attention back to the screen. With Trill for a distraction, he had no idea what the storyline was.

He lifted their hands up to his lips and kissed the back of her hand, and smiled at her indrawn breath. "I want you to sleep in my arms tonight." The couch under them was a hide-a-bed, but he wouldn't tell her, not wanting her to have the choice of sleeping apart. If she insisted on sleeping on the couch, he'd tell her and take it himself.

Oh, he'd give in and let her fall asleep on her side of the bed, if she wanted, because he was pretty sure she'd end up cuddled next to him again.

She bit her lip. "What are you asking?"

"Just sleep. I really liked waking up this morning with you snuggled against me."

A blush covered her cheeks and she dropped her gaze. "But I'm half a whale."

He lifted her chin with a finger. "Trill, you're not in any way related to a whale. I think of you as a beautiful woman who happens to be nurturing a baby."

One corner of her mouth twitched.

"You're incredibly brave. You could have done what Wolf suggested, but instead, you're risking your life to keep this baby alive."

She rubbed her belly. "He's part of me. He deserves to live, to grow up."

He kissed her cheek. "That's one of the things I like about you. So, what do you say? Can I hold you while we sleep?"

She stared at him. "Okay." Trill lowered her gaze. "I liked it, too."

The ending credits rolled on the screen as he turned the TV off. He didn't know who they'd revealed as the killer and didn't care.

He stood and tugged her to her feet. "Why don't you go get ready for bed and I'll join you shortly?" It was a bit early, but maybe they would end up talking in the dark.

He hadn't scried a premonition that morning, so he settled back on the couch and closed his eyes, taking deep breaths. He concentrated on Trill. An image materialized of her bent over a pool table, pool stick in her hands as she lined up a shot. He looked forward to seeing that broad smile on her face for real. He hadn't checked into the amenities of the park, but would be happy to explore them with her.

Apparently, they would be safe for another day.

Water ran in the bathroom sink and he waited a few minutes more, then headed to the bedroom. Trill lay near the center of the bed, huddled under the blankets. He was relieved she hadn't changed her mind.

He hurried through getting ready for bed and stripped to his boxers. He hesitated before dropping his t-shirt into the laundry basket. Maybe he should put it back on. Nah. He wanted to be as close to Trill as possible.

In the bedroom, he flipped the light switch, plunging the room into darkness. He crept the few steps to the bed and slipped under the covers, scooting until his chest touched Trill's back. He slid one arm under her pillow, and wrapped the other around her waist, settling his hand against her belly, the same material covering it as the nightgown she'd worn the night before. His bare legs touched her slightly warmer ones. This felt even better, more right, than last time. He cradled her. A tingle of energy passed from her. It should have heightened his awareness of her, but instead, it relaxed him. Maybe he wouldn't try to have a conversation after all.

"Good night, Trill."

"G'night, Adam."

He buried his nose in her hair and hoped he dreamed about all the ways he wanted to pleasure this beautiful woman.

Chapter 10

Trill dragged in a long breath of Adam. She was already warm, but his closeness made her downright toasty. Her nose was planted against his chest and her arm hung over his side. His leg rested between hers. If her tummy had been smaller, she'd probably feel something else, too.

In the night, she'd gotten up to use the bathroom, and when she'd crawled back into bed, in his sleep he gathered her into his arms. Front to front.

His chest rumbled against her cheek. "I wondered how long it would be before you woke up."

She'd planned on waking up and dressing before he stirred. "How long have you been awake?"

"About a half-hour."

Her heart thumped in a rapid beat. She'd slide away to disentangle herself from him, but she'd probably only entice him more. "And you just stayed here?"

"I couldn't convince myself to let you go." He stuck a finger under her chin and lifted her face to him. Those ice blue eyes melted her. "Good morning." He kissed her.

Her breath caught in her throat. She couldn't figure out where her left arm was, but the one draped over his waist seemed to have a life of its own as her hand rubbed up his torso, around the back of his neck and tunneled into his hair.

He groaned and deepened the kiss. His hand slid down

her back and snuggled her tighter against him, her rounded stomach against his firm, flat abs. Probably not at all what he was used to.

He peppered kisses across her cheek and his breath fanned her ear. "I want to make love with you."

She stared at him. "But I'm—"

"Beautiful." His expression was so…earnest. Like this meant everything to him.

She bit her lip. "I don't know if I can."

His cheeks tinged pink. "I Googled pregnant sex, and they gave position suggestions."

Her mouth dropped open and she snapped it shut. Oh, my goodness.

He kissed her cheek. "I'm clean. I haven't had sex in over a year and got tested six months ago."

And she'd gotten tested during her prenatal checkup and he'd heard the results. She'd been so relieved she hadn't caught something from Art during however much unprotected sex they'd had, that she hadn't thought about Adam hearing the same information.

He must have been thinking about it for a while. And she—really hadn't been, but his kisses made her want so much more than she'd had the last couple of years, at least the ones she remembered.

"Okay."

He grinned and gave her a quick kiss. "When you're ready, you're on top."

She bit her lip. "I need to use the bathroom first." How embarrassing was that?

He grinned. "You know where to find me." He shuffled under the blankets and tossed his boxers on the floor.

Trill fled to the bathroom, emptied her bladder and brushed her teeth. Her hair was a mess, but there was no sense in brushing it. She rubbed circles over her belly, and had no idea how Adam could see past it. She drew in a deep breath, marched back to the bedroom, and stopped beside the bed.

Adam's gaze was on her face. He didn't say anything, maybe not wanting to influence her decision. He was naked under the blankets, waiting for her to join him. She could grab clothes and go back into the bathroom and he wouldn't stop her, wouldn't yell at her, wouldn't be angry at her.

That's what decided her. He wouldn't coerce her. She reached under her nightgown, tugged down her panties, and stepped out of them when they hit her feet.

His breathing quickened, and his pale blue eyes became almost silvery.

She bunched up the bottom of her nightgown in her hands, then yanked it over her head, dropping it on the floor. Now, it was his decision. He could see what he was getting.

"Trill, you're beautiful." He flipped back the blankets, leaving himself covered, but giving her an unspoken invitation.

She climbed into the bed and he covered her, then kissed her neck and nibbled on her ear, giving her a full body shiver. His lips traveled along her jaw and found her lips. As he invaded her senses, his hand skimmed the side of her tummy and cupped her breast. His thumb rubbed her nipple and she soared through the roof, not realizing how sensitive it had gotten. She groaned and shifted. If she wasn't totally sure before, she was all onboard now.

She lifted up, and settled down around his hips. But now, she couldn't easily reach his lips.

His hand had followed her breast and the other snaked between them, eliciting a hum from her as his fingers worked magic. She gazed down, only catching his tanned hand against her naturally brown skin. The sight of his thumb rolling over her nipple edged up the tingles coursing through her. She couldn't see beyond her belly to watch his other hand, but oh, what it did to her. And the insistent bumping of his hard length against the bottom of her belly made her ache for it to find a home.

She slid one hand up his muscled torso and feathered her fingers over his nipple as the other reached under and grasped him. He groaned. His gaze dropped to her guiding hand as she lowered herself onto him, and they moaned in unison.

***

Adam woke for the second time that morning, and glanced at the clock. Okay. Morning ended ten minutes ago. Trill must be starved.

This time, having her tucked in beside him was better than earlier. They were both naked. The baby bump trapped between them was a little awkward, but he wouldn't trade it for anything. One of his arms circled the back of her neck with his hand resting on her shoulder. The other hand rubbed her tummy. Even while he slept, he'd tried to comfort Lucas.

Although he'd forced a premonition the night before, he needed to get on track for the morning visions. He closed his eyes, and dove forward through time, with his thoughts on Trill. He found her in this room, darkened windows, her eyes closed, lips parted and an expression of bliss. Yes. He'd make sure that happened again. And again.

A hand touched his cheek. "What's that grin for?"

His grin widened as he opened his eyes. "Just having a vision of a vision."

Her eyebrows scrunch. "What?"

"I forced a premonition. It showed you. Naked. In here."

She bit her lip. "Did you have a vision like that before we did this?"

He shook his head. "No. I've never had any

premonitions that showed naked women."

"I'm glad."

He sat up. "How about you shower while I make breakfast? Or would you prefer lunch?"

Her head swung to the clock. "Is it really twelve-twenty?"

"Yep. So, which is it?"

"Breakfast."

He climbed out of bed and helped Trill up, but he couldn't let her go yet. He kissed her to the point that he wanted to take her back to bed, but he wouldn't. She needed sustenance. "Now go while I still have some willpower."

Twenty minutes later, he set the table, poured orange juice for Trill and coffee for him. They'd purchased decaf, but he'd already brewed the regular before he remembered. He pulled the Fig Newtons out of the cupboard and set them on the table.

Trill entered the little kitchen and he couldn't resist giving her a kiss. Making love had launched him from falling-in-love to head-over-heels in-love. She needed more spontaneous kisses, so that when he kissed her for no apparent reason, she didn't seem startled by it.

She scanned the kitchen. "I smell food, but I don't see any. Did I take too long and you ate it all?"

"It's staying warm in the oven. Have a seat while I get it." He placed butter and maple syrup on the table, then picked up potholders and retrieved two plates from the oven.

She grinned. "Oh, I love chocolate chip pancakes."

She speared three sausage links and slid them off the fork with her knife, then took a pancake, poured syrup over it, and repeated with a second pancake.

Adam helped himself to food. "I think, after I shower, we should explore the amenities here. I challenge you to a game of pool."

She cut a sausage and held it halfway to her mouth. "What else do they have?"

"I have no idea. I only know there's a pool table because I saw you playing in a vision last night."

She grinned. "Did I win?"

"I only saw you lining up a shot. I guess we'll see." Some things he didn't want to know ahead of time. "Are you any good?"

She shrugged. "There's a table at the rec center on the reservation. Wolf and I used to play a lot. It's been at least a couple of years since I played. How about you?"

He kept his eyes on his plate. "My dad had a billiard room. Two tables. Art used to challenge me, but he'd only play if we made bets. Once I started winning most of the time, he stopped playing with me." Sometimes, bets were cash, but most of the time, it was for chores or some kind of dare.

"So, you're a pool shark?"

He chuckled. "Better than Art, anyway." He glanced at her, and wished he hadn't mentioned Art. She rubbed her belly and he wondered if she thought about what Art wanted to do to her.

After they finished eating, Adam showered while Trill cleaned up the kitchen.

Once dressed, he grabbed their coats. Trill swiped a couple of Newtons, and they headed out. They decided to walk to the buildings behind the office, following a previous snow packed path cutting between trailers.

They stopped at the closest building, the largest, and Adam swung the door open. Trill strolled in first and the lights flickered on. An air hockey table stood to their left. Two pool tables sat in front of them, and various pool sticks lined the right wall in a rack. At the far end of the room, a large screen TV was mounted on the wall and several couches and chairs faced it. Two vending machines sat side-by-side halfway down the left wall, one held cold drinks and the other snacks.

He grabbed Trill's hand. "Let's come back and play pool after we check out the other buildings."

"Okay."

They passed a fenced-in covered pool. Too bad it wasn't summer. He'd love to play in the water with Trill. Maybe they could return when it was warm. Whoa! They might not be together after the danger was past. After the baby was born. But he hoped so.

She tugged his hand, and he realized he'd stopped. "Ah, sorry. I was just thinking about swimming with you."

She giggled. "We're not swimming today." She tugged again and he followed her to the building behind the pool. She opened the door and he followed her in. A large hot tub filled the space and benches lined two walls.

He imagined some time in the hot tub might help her relax and he could make her crave him before they hurried back to their RV. Maybe after dinner. He whispered in her ear. "You could wear a t-shirt and panties in there." Maybe he'd talk her out of the panties.

She sighed. "I can't. It's in the pamphlet the doctor gave me. Hot tubs can harm the baby."

And that daydream furled up in smoke. "Let's see what's in the last building."

It was a longer trek to the building near the pond. Or maybe it was a lake. At what size did a body of water become a lake?

He tried to twist the doorknob, but it was locked. He shielded his eyes and peeked in the window. Paddles and oars filled tall barrels, and lifejackets were stacked on shelves. Sort of a boathouse. He stared out at the patchy ice and water. Nearby, overturned canoes and kayaks with snow covering them sat stacked in racks. "I guess we won't be using these amenities either."

She took his hand. "Let's go to the office. I saw a rack with flyers for attractions. Some of them must be open this time of year."

"Wait!" He held his hand over the lock until it gave a satisfying click. He opened the door far enough to peak inside. The wooden floor appeared to have been swept. A stepstool leaned against the far wall.

He closed the door and faced her. "This might be a place you can hide if Art finds us here. I'm leaving it unlocked, but you can lock it from inside."

Trill bit her lip and nodded. "I keep trying to forget about him."

Adam hugged her. He hated dampening her mood.

The office was empty when they entered. Adam followed Trill to the info rack. He plucked out flyer after flyer and returned them when he found each business closed in October.

She held one up. "Here's one that's open all year round. It's an art museum." Her eyes met his. "Do you like checking out art?"

The door opened and Beth entered. "Hey, you two. Looking for stuff to do?"

"Yeah." Adam smiled at Trill. "We'll probably spend most of our time in the RV, but we want to get out a bit, too."

He loved the blush that fanned her cheeks, and gave one a kiss. That should make Beth think they were making this a honeymoon, but he did it more for himself. He couldn't help it.

Beth stopped beside them. "Normally, I'd recommend renting snowmobiles or cross-country skis, but I don't think that will work for you two." She stepped to the side and extracted a flyer from the rack. "There's the historical society. It's a pretty interesting history." She flipped the flyer over. "And if you like old houses, they've got two associated with them." She plucked out another flyer. "And there's the outlet mall."

Beth stepped back. "And on Saturday, the town is having its winter festival. Ice sculptures, skating races, Christmas tree throwing—"

"People throw Christmas trees for fun?" Adam asked.

"People save their trees and bring them to the festival. There's a knack to it. The festival's in the big field on the other side of downtown."

He raised his brows and gazed at Trill. "What do you think?"

"It sounds like fun." She grinned. "Are you going to throw a tree?"

"Let's just wait and see what it's all about." He didn't want to hurt himself right when he needed to save Trill.

Beth stuffed her hands in her pockets. "There's also the Langdon Tavern. It's about a hundred-fifty years old. Rustic atmosphere and they have the best food. That's along Main St." She glanced at the rack. "Well, I've got to get some stuff done." She scooted behind the counter and sat at the desk under the window.

Trill picked up a couple more flyers and they left.

He held her hand on the walk back to the RV. They took the road this time. "Why don't we checkout the downtown area and eat dinner at that tavern?"

"That sounds nice."

It would be their first date. After they'd already made love. The only food they'd eaten out had been what they'd grabbed on the run at fast food chains.

He wouldn't tell Trill, but he'd packed a small bag with a few clothes and put it in the trunk, just in case Art found them while they were out.

Chapter 11

Trill kissed Adam's chest. She hadn't known how enjoyable it was to wake up in a man's arms. Only one of her boyfriends had ever stayed until morning, and he'd always rolled away from her after they had sex. And that's all it had been. After making love with Adam for nearly two weeks, she now knew the difference.

He treated her as if she was the most important person in the world. Whenever he was near, he touched her, as if he had to. He always held her hand when they walked. Often when she cooked, he came up behind her, his chest against her back, and kissed the side of her head. If they watched TV, he snuggled her close or swung her legs over his lap and rubbed her feet. Touching had become important to her, too.

She ran a hand over her growing belly. It was amazing how much larger it was in a month's time. Lucas moved around more, too, with fluttery little kicks. It wouldn't be long before it would feel like he played soccer inside her.

Adam kissed her forehead. "Morning, beautiful."

Except for that first time, they hadn't made love in the morning. Every night and some afternoons made up for that.

He sat up, and closed his eyes. Like every morning, he forced a premonition. She put her hand on his thigh and waited. They ended up doing whatever the premonition had showed. It was strange to not think about it, but follow what he'd seen. The winter festival, window shopping, museums. They'd talked about all the places, but let the vision determine when they did them. Their time at the RV park had been like a honeymoon, or at least a vacation.

She'd fallen more and more in love with Adam. He showed his love in his concern for her comfort, doing things that made her happy or excited, and making her safety his priority. She'd shared how difficult it had been when her mother died and father left, something she'd only talked to Wolf about. He told her about how lost he'd been when his mother died, and after that, the best times were when he spent a few weeks in the summer with his mother's parents.

Adam's thigh tensed and the corners of his lips dipped down. Tears leaked from his closed eyes. No! This wasn't a happy vision. She'd stopped feeling scared. Now it rushed back. Again, her life was threatened, with Adam her only ally.

Finally, he opened his watery eyes. "We have to leave, now."

He jumped out of bed, and yanked her to her feet. The suitcase she'd never really unpacked lay on the dresser. She threw her dirty clothes on top of the clean clothes, and packed up the bathroom without brushing her teeth or hair.

Her bag and Adam's were already gone. In the kitchen, she put on her shoes and coat. He hurried inside and hugged her. "I'm sorry."

She didn't know what he was sorry about. She'd be dead already if not for him.

She gazed around the little piece of heaven she'd grown to love. "What about all the food?"

He dropped the RV key on the table. "Once we're on the road, I'll call the office about the food and where the key is."

They got in the car and before she could buckle up, he tore down the lane and around the turn leading to the road. A roar of an engine gave warning before a black car rounded the corner and headed for them. No! It had to be Art barreling into the park. As the BMW approached the bridge, it skidded sideways, coming to an abrupt stop, blocking their path.

If Adam was going to have premonitions, couldn't he get them a day before something bad would happen?

They wouldn't be able to leave without moving the car. The far door opened and a man got out. Art. No surprise. She didn't want Adam to get hurt, and she couldn't let Art take her. Trill grabbed Adam's arm. "You can't go out there."

He pried her fingers off his arm. "Honey, I don't have a choice. There's no other way out of here and I'm not letting Art near this car so he can take you. When I get out, lock the doors and slide to the driver's seat." He stepped out and closed the door and she hit the lock button.

She was trapped in the car. Art could get in if he broke the window, but he'd have to go through Adam to do it.

Adam and Art stood a foot from each other, anger on both their faces. Her heart raced. Art was so much bigger than Adam. Adam would have to be an expert in self-defense to overcome Art's bulk.

Art's fist rammed into Adam's stomach. As he doubled over with a grunt, Art swung his knuckles into Adam's jaw. He dropped onto his side facing away from her. She didn't know if he was unconscious.

Maybe she could draw Art away from Adam if she backed up and drove around the park. With her back against the door, she drew her left knee up beside her belly and thrust her foot over the console. She did the same with the other leg. Thrusting against the door's armrest she straightened her body, and slid into the driver's seat, dropping her legs to the floor.

Art's gaze met hers and her body chilled. If he got his hands on her, it wouldn't take long for the condition to be permanent. He could break into the car. If she wasn't pregnant she could have outrun him, but now she was a beached whale.

Art took slow steps toward the car. Toward her. His evil grin caused shivers to run up her spine. He yanked the door handle. "Open the door!"

She shook her head. Her voice had locked up.

He pointed at her stomach. "That baby is mine. You can't keep me from it."

Lucas kicked twice, as if he understood the danger. She rubbed her tummy. Art hadn't said, "mine, too" or "ours." He thought of Lucas as his possession.

Sooner or later he'd get inside. She had to back up now. She grabbed the gear shift.

Art jerked and his head snapped up. He roared and spun around. Flames licked at the edges of a hole in his shirt. More and more raw flesh was revealed as the fire burned at the edges of the shirt. He was in pain, but he wasn't down.

Maybe she could freeze him from the back. She sensed that if she held his arm when she tried to freeze him, it would only freeze his arm. It had to start in his torso. Her gaze darted to the side as Adam struggled to his feet. He held his palms a few inches apart and flames appeared between them. He balanced the fire in one hand and lobbed it at Art. They were close enough that Art didn't have much time to react. He dove to the right, but the fireball caught him in the shoulder.

Maybe she could have rammed the other car, but sitting perpendicular, she'd do more damage to Adam's car. And then there was the fact that the brothers fought between the cars.

Art's punches had more impact, but Adam was lighter on his feet. Adam was too busy defending himself to take the time to make another fireball.

Maybe she should try to freeze Art. His back was to her. If he didn't hear the door open, she might be able to sneak up on him, and put her hand on his back.

Trill pulled the door handle and waited. No reaction from the guys. She nudged the door open a bit. Still nothing. She opened the door wide enough to get out, and stood. She could still jump back inside and lock it.

Adam glanced at her and quickly away. He was probably sending her messages to get back in the car, but he couldn't say anything or it would draw attention to her. She crept behind Art and slapped her palm against his back. With the deep burn, the freeze would probably help him before stopping him.

He stiffened and swung around, grabbing her wrist. "Got yah!"

She slammed her other hand onto his chest. Adam rocked him with a fist to the jaw which made her sidestep to stay on her feet and keep her hand on Art's chest.

Art lifted his other hand and it paused inches from the hand on his chest. The freeze must have taken hold.

Adam pried Art's fingers off her reddened wrist, and shoved him over. He fell like a downed redwood. Adam dragged him to the edge of the road, then ran to Art's car and peeked inside. "The keys are here. Trill, get back in the car and I'll move this."

She hurried back to Adam's car, and climbed into the driver's seat. Adam made a sharp turn and parallel parked the car half off the road. She drove forward, waiting for Adam to jump in.

He got out of Art's car, took out his knife and punch a hole in one tire, then threw the keys into the river. He leaned over his brother. "Stay away from Trill."

He raced to his car and jumped in. "Go!"

She peeled out of the driveway and headed for the

highway.

He buckled his seatbelt. "When I tell you to stay in the car. Do. Not. Leave. It." He drew in and huffed out two breaths. "Art had his murdering hands on you. That could have easily gone the other way."

She glanced at him and back to the road. She'd never seen him angry before. "But, Adam, he could have killed you."

"He's my brother. He wouldn't kill me."

She tightened her grip on the steering wheel. "You stopped him twice already. You don't think he's angry enough to kill you?"

Adam rubbed a hand down his face and dropped his head against the headrest. "I don't know. I wouldn't kill him."

She shook her head. "Seriously? That's your logic? How many things has he done in the past six months, or his entire life, that you wouldn't do? How can you think that he wouldn't add killing his brother?"

He rubbed his face again. "You're right. I don't know. In the two premonitions I was in, he knocked me unconscious. I assumed that's all he would do to me."

She dropped her shoulders, letting the tension leave them. "Where are we going?"

He sighed. "I don't know. Head north for now." He slammed his fist on the dash. "How did he find us this time?"

"I wish I knew."

They lapsed into silence.

After driving for ten minutes a thought struck Trill and she giggled.

Adam squinted at her. "Are you all right?"

She giggled more. "Yes. I just realized we're fire and ice."

He grinned. "I guess opposites attract."

***

Adam and Trill stopped at a fast food restaurant for breakfast sandwiches and he took over driving. He couldn't drive aimlessly. They had to do something different because Art would find them again. It had taken longer this time than last, but it had still happened. And maybe next time they wouldn't be as lucky.

They needed help. Others with abilities who understood what they were up against and had additional weapons. Like Jamie's family. He couldn't see them helping him. Not with Jamie believing he participated in her kidnapping.

There wasn't another choice, though. Hopefully, they'd help for Trill's sake. They wouldn't turn away a pregnant woman who would be killed to increase the powers of an evil man. If he had to, he'd leave her with them and drive away. It would be one of the hardest things he ever did, but he'd do it to keep Trill and her baby alive.

He stopped on the side of the road and entered the town of Rawlins, Massachusetts into his GPS. He didn't know where Jamie or her family lived, but Rawlins was small.

Trill grabbed his hand. "You figured out somewhere we can hide?"

He rubbed the back of his neck and got on the road. "Yeah. Let's just hope the people there will help us."

He had to tell her about the month he'd spent with Jamie. He hoped she didn't hate him or become afraid of him once he told her the details.

He glanced at her and squeezed her hand. "We're going to Rawlins. I'll talk to Jamie Ballard's family. She and I were imprisoned together for about a month. My father ordered me to his office, threw me into a basement room and locked the door. Turned out, he'd already kidnapped Jamie, and put her in the same room. I didn't let on I was related to the man who imprisoned us, so now Jamie and her whole family think I was involved in it."

"Oh, Adam. Why did he do that?"

He sucked in a breath and let it out slowly. "Jamie and I were betrothed when we were little. We would have been married by now if her parents hadn't died and she got adopted."

Trill touched his leg. "Oh, how sad for her. How old was she?"

"Two. It was the best thing that ever happened to her. She wouldn't have turned out to be the sweet woman she is if they'd lived."

"Maybe. Look how good you turned out with your horrible father."

He patted her hand. She made him feel like a decent person. "My mom made all the difference with me. Anyway, Dad still tried to get us together by throwing me at her in college. It didn't work."

"So, he figured if it was the two of you against your captors, she might fall for you?"

"That's what I thought his intent was, but Art thinks Dad just wanted me to get her pregnant."

Trill yanked her hand away. "Oh. So, you, um—"

"No. She already had a boyfriend. She realized she was pregnant about three weeks into our imprisonment. Dad exploded over that, and brought in a doctor to abort her."

She rubbed her tummy. "Poor girl. I can't imagine having that forced on someone."

"I don't know how she did it, but it didn't happen."

"That's a relief."

"Yeah. But it didn't end well for me when her family rescued her."

She squeezed his arm. "And that's who we're going to for help?"

He glanced at her. "Yeah. Crazy, huh?"

***

After spending the night at a cheap chain motel off the highway, they rolled into Rawlins before lunch. Adam took Trill's hand. Her life depended on him getting this right.

He scanned the buildings in the small town center. There, that looked promising. "Ballard Real Estate and Rentals. We should be able to find them through that office. But first, let's get you some lunch."

A couple of blocks up, he spotted two restaurants across from each other, and pulled to the curb. "Which do you want? The Black Kettle Restaurant or Cozy Corner Diner." He waited for her answer as her gaze darted between the buildings.

She shifted. "You choose. My priority is the bathroom."

He choked off a chuckle. She wouldn't react well to that. He shifted the car to drive and headed to the parking lot for The Black Kettle, assuming that a restaurant had a more varied menu than a diner for Trill to select from.

They made their way inside and the hostess seated them. Adam couldn't help but notice how many of the customers surreptitiously watched them. Must be the small town atmosphere. During the meal, he put off thinking about the coming confrontation, and talked about anything but that with Trill. He didn't want her to worry that the Ballard's would send them away.

Adam couldn't delay any longer, and his frayed nerves were at their limit. He escorted Trill back to the car and drove to the Ballard building, parking in the lot beside it. He sucked in a breath and let it out. He tried another. It didn't help. "Let's get this over with."

He got out of the car and opened Trill's door, taking her

hand to assist.

She kissed his cheek. "It's going to be all right."

He touched his forehead to hers. "I hope so." It had to be. Or he'd lose her.

She laced her fingers through his and they strode up the walk. He held the door open and she preceded him inside.

A man, probably in his fifties, sat at a desk about ten feet in front of the door, and studied them. He stood. "Hi. I'm Reese Ballard. Are you two looking for a home?"

Adam stepped forward. "No. We need help."

Reese frowned. "Are you lost?"

"No. This is Trill Song, and I'm Adam Richards."

Reese's expression instantly changed to anger. Yeah, Reese knew who he was.

Reese stepped around the desk, his hands fisted at his sides. "Get out of my town. I don't want you anywhere near my daughter."

Adam drew in a breath. "I'm not interested in Jamie. We need help. My brother is trying to kill Trill, and he keeps finding us."

Reese leaned against the desk and crossed his arms. "And why should I care?"

Adam knew this would be hard, but he hadn't expected the first person they ran into would be Jamie's father. He was probably as hard to convince as Jamie's boyfriend would be. "Because you wouldn't want to see an innocent woman die, if you can save her."

Reese's gaze settled on Trill. Adam was ready to scream, "Say something," when Reese straightened, and relaxed his arms. "Come back to my office and we'll talk."

Adam let out a breath as he followed Reese, his hand still holding Trill's. One small hurdle leaped.

Reese sat behind a desk, and Adam and Trill sat in the two chairs facing it.

Adam closed his eyes, willing himself to stay calm, glad that he'd had months of therapy to bolster his courage. He stared into Reese's eyes, begging him to believe what he said. "I was a prisoner in that basement just as much as Jamie was. My father threw me in there and I had no idea she was there until I saw her. The only advantage I had was that I knew he wouldn't kill us."

Reese crossed his arms. "You didn't tell her it was your father who kidnapped both of you."

Adam dropped his gaze, then glanced again at Reese. "No, I didn't. I figured he was making a last ditch effort to get us together, that the forced adversity would draw us together." Adam squinted. "I had no control over anything that happened outside of that room."

He assumed Jamie had told her family everything that had happened while she was imprisoned, as well as that he hadn't touched her.

Reese pressed his lips together. "When Theron and Jason rescued Jamie, you wouldn't let her go."

Adam's face heated, and he glanced at Trill, who only seemed to show curiosity. "Yeah, well. It was a sudden shock that she was being taken from me." He glanced at Trill again, before returning his gaze to Reese. "I had a breakdown." He huffed. "I spent the next month in a psych ward." Maybe he should have told Trill all of this sometime in the past weeks. At least before revealing it all to a stranger in front of her.

Reese narrowed his eyes.

Adam lifted his hand up. "Hey, I'm okay now. I spent six months talking to a court appointed psychologist."

Adam gazed back at Trill. She didn't appear to be horrified.

Reese nodded toward Trill. "So, what's your story?"

Adam's shoulders relaxed. He'd gotten over another hurdle.

"Adam saved my life. Art conceived this baby"—she patted her tummy—"to gain power. Now, he needs to kill me and the baby to finish it."

Adam took Trill's hand, noticing Reese following the action. "I had a premonition. In it, my brother cut the baby out of Trill, and did a power transfer ritual. He killed Trill and left the baby to die." Adam continued to explain how he'd found Trill and how Art had tracked them down three times.

Adam rubbed the back of his neck. "I don't know how he found us. I'm afraid of what will happen the next time."

Reese stared at Adam. "So, you're protecting Art's baby?"

"It's not his anymore. And I'm protecting Trill, too." He couldn't keep the anger from his voice.

Trill squeezed his fingers, and he returned the gesture.

Reese leaned back in his chair and laced his fingers on his chest. His gaze bounced between Adam and Trill. It was like those times he sat in front of the principal. Reese scribbled on a small pad, tore the paper off and handed it to Adam. "Come to my house at six o'clock."

Adam glanced at the address on the note.

"I'll contact Jason and Theron. We'll all have dinner and discuss if we'll protect Trill and maybe how to do it. If we do help, it won't be for you, but for her."

Adam relaxed his shoulders. "I understand."

Reese stood. Adam took his cue and got to his feet, helping Trill up.

Adam held out his hand. "Thank you."

Reese hesitated for a moment before shaking Adam's hand.

Reese hadn't agreed yet, and Jamie's boyfriend and brother still had to hear Trill and Adam's story and decide. He hadn't made a good first impression with those two.

Chapter 12

Trill's knees shook as Adam helped her from the car he'd parked at the curb. She stared up at the Ballard mansion. It should be a museum, not a home. It had to be more than a hundred-fifty years old. A porch ran the length of the house with tall, thick columns supporting the roof over it. She'd bet no one ever sat in the chairs grouped around two tables. Dark gray shutters lined the sides of the many windows, against the lighter gray of the wood siding.

Several cars sat in the circular driveway. Yes, the gang was all there. This family wasn't happy with Adam, so she feared what would happen inside. Her brave Adam. She didn't think she could have begged for help from people who thought she'd wronged them. More than anything, this told her how much Adam cared for her and Lucas.

He stared into her eyes, concern in his own. "Are you ready?"

She kissed his cheek, and smiled. "Thank you. This must be so hard for you."

He pulled her close and whispered. "I'd do anything to keep you and Lucas safe." He leaned back and stared at her. "I need you to promise something. If they say the only way they'll help you is if I leave, you have to let me go."

She shook her head. "No. I can't do that. If they won't accept you, then I'm leaving, too."

He held her tight. "Trill, please. I can't protect you by myself any longer. I need you and Lucas to live. I can find you after. Promise me."

She touched his face, wavy through the tears. "All right. But I'm going to try my hardest to make sure they take you, too."

He let out a long breath, twisted away, and took her hand. "Let's get this show on the road."

They climbed the steps and their heels thudded across the wooden porch. Adam rang the doorbell, and too quickly the door opened.

A high school age girl stood in front of them and half turned away. "They're here!"

Reese stormed up to the door and Trill squished into Adam's side, his arm coming protectively around her.

Reese glared at the young woman. "Abby, you were supposed to stay upstairs until you were called down for dinner."

"But, Dad, you trusted them enough to let them come." She stalked away, not taking the stairs.

Trill stared after her, then gazed at Reese. "She looks like a handful."

Reese rubbed his temples. "Not often, thank God." He stepped back. "Come on in. Dinner's almost set in the formal dining room."

Formal? Like there was also an informal dining room? They stepped into a foyer. She couldn't call it an entry area. Right and left were living rooms, the right one smaller and cozy with a big screen television.

Past those, Reese opened a door. A closet. "Let me take your coats."

She handed hers over. Across from them, an empty dining room held a huge table with twelve chairs. It seemed pretty formal to her, but obviously not where they were eating.

The closet door clicked closed and Trill faced Reese. He pointed at the next door. "There's a bathroom."

They stepped into a room full of people. The formal dining room. A table twice as long as the other one took up most of the space. Two sideboards sat side-by-side on the left wall. Only about half the table was set with plates, and covered dishes sat in the center. On the right side of the room, several people stood talking, but silenced when she and Adam entered.

A pregnant woman with wavy dark hair could probably have her baby any minute. The man stepped in front of her and poised himself to strike. She had to be Jamie. A man, who had to be Jamie's brother, pulled a woman with golden eyes into his side. Abby stood beside an older woman, probably her mother.

A young college age man sat sideways on a captain's chair, his legs over the arm and an elbow on the back. The young man rolled his eyes. "Another one?"

Trill had no idea what that meant.

Reese squinted at the man. "Adam, Trill, that rude young man is my son, Tony. Beside him are my wife, Kathleen, and daughter, Abby." He pointed at the woman who had worked her way to the front of her bodyguard, and now was wrapped in his arms. "My daughter, Jamie, and her husband, Theron." He pointed at the last couple. "My son, Jason, and his wife, Shauna."

He pulled out a chair to the left of the head of the table. "Why don't we sit down and eat?"

Kathleen settled into the chair Reese stood behind, and he sat at the head of the table. Abby plopped into the chair on his other side, with her oldest brother beside her. The two women sat together with Theron on the end. Tony relaxed beside his mother, and Trill took her place beside him, with

Adam sitting next to her. She was relieved they hadn't been separated. Everyone had wary expressions, except for that Theron guy, who glared at Adam.

A huge bowl of salad, and another of rolls passed hand-to-hand, and Kathleen and Jamie dished up pieces of lasagna from two huge baking pans. Trill wasn't sure if she'd be able to eat with the nervous quiver in her stomach.

Once everyone was served, Jamie leaned in close to Shauna. "How do you feel?"

Trill didn't think she was supposed to hear.

"Just a bit nauseous. No real morning sickness."

Jamie grimaced. "Lucky you. Mine lasted way too long." She glanced at Trill. "What about you?"

Trill startled. Maybe they weren't having a secret conversation. "Uh. I don't remember."

Both women's eyebrows rose.

Adam rubbed her thigh. "My brother had her under a controlling spell. Once I broke the spell, she didn't remember anything from that time."

Jamie glared at Reese. "Dad, you didn't tell us that part."

Reese shrugged. "I figured it would all come out tonight."

Trill took a bite of the lasagna, hoping it would remind the others to eat, and remove herself from the center of attention. Not that it would work for long since she and Adam were there for help.

Adam cleared his throat. He gazed across the table at Jamie. "Before we start with figuring out how to rescue Trill, I want to apologize to Jamie."

Jamie bit her lip, and Theron leaned into her.

"I was taken by surprise by my father, and kidnapped, too. That part was real. I decided to go along with it by not telling you who he was to me. All my life, he wanted the two of us to get together." He shrugged. "So, I thought I'd give it one last shot. I'm sorry I didn't tell you the truth."

Theron glared. "Why aren't you in prison like your father?"

Poor Adam. He was going through this for her. He probably wished he could have given Jamie the apology in private, but that scary husband of hers wouldn't let Adam anywhere near her.

"Because my father told the police how he kidnapped me." Adam blew out a long breath. "And Jamie, I didn't know he expected me to get you pregnant, not until Art taunted me about how he could do it better."

Jamie gasped. "That's what you two talked about? Why didn't you tell me?"

"I was afraid of how you'd react to me." Adam glanced at Theron. "And you don't have to worry about me. I've had six months of visits to a psychologist. I'm over the obsession."

Theron glared. "I'm still keeping my eye on you."

Tony had been the only one to continue eating through Adam's speech. "Man, that's some messed up stuff."

Trill squeezed Adam's hand. He gazed at her, and she gave him a small smile. It had to have been harder saying all that to Jamie than what he'd told her father. And in front of her whole family.

Adam's gaze traveled over everyone at the table. "I know you don't owe me anything, but I would really appreciate it if you could help me save Trill." His eyes stopped on her. Again, he scanned the others. "In case Reese missed something, let me recap." He described what they'd been through, and as with Reese, left out the part about Lucas' spirit. She was glad because it seemed too personal.

Everyone had resumed eating while Adam talked.

"I think I know how he's finding her," Kathleen said. "He's tracking his baby, like Theron can sense Jamie through their baby."

Adam stiffened. "Lucas is not his baby anymore." Trill loved how protective he was.

Kathleen sighed. "The baby still carries your brother's genes."

"Fine," Adam huffed. "So, how do we prevent Art from finding him? I figured the medicine bags Trill and I wear would do it."

"Maybe before you split it, the original medicine bag might have shielded the baby, too," Kathleen said.

Adam's eyes widened. "I put you at risk." He reached under his shirt. "We should put this back into your bag."

She slowly shook her head. "You need to be hidden, too. This was my idea, and Gram thought it would work."

"I've got an idea," Kathleen said. This woman seemed to know a lot about spells and magic. "Jason, how many more of those medallions do you have upstairs?"

Jason leaned forward. "I don't know. Do you want me to check and bring one down?"

"Yes. Fetch two, if you've got them. I'm going to get my spell book." She left the room.

Reese slid back his chair. "Let's move to the other end of the table. Abby, Tony, please clear the dishes."

Abby rose and crossed her arms. "But, Dad. I don't want to miss anything."

Reese narrowed his eyes. "Then get started. And don't forget to load them into the dishwasher."

Kathleen returned with a one inch thick leather-bound book, a pad of paper and pen. Reese had taken the opposite head of the table and she sat in the seat beside him. "Trill, sit here." She patted the chair beside her.

Adam dropped into the chair next to her. She'd never had such a large group of people willing to help her with anything before. There'd always been Gram and Wolf, but no one outside the family until Adam, and now all these people.

Jason strode in and sat beside Shauna, then dropped two silver chains in front of his mother. "I only found one medallion, but I also had an eagle necklace."

Trill clasped her hands. "The eagle is mystical for my people."

Kathleen picked up one chain. "Then we'll use that one." She unhooked the clasp, and slid the medallion off, then opened the other necklace and hooked the two together. She held the ends up and stood. "Trill, let me see if this fits you. Can you stand?"

Trill scooted her chair back and stood. Kathleen reached around Trill's waist and grabbed one end of the chain and circled it around Trill. Or where her waist used to be.

Trill twisted to peek over her shoulder as Kathleen attached the second clasp to one of the chain loops.

"There. And there's still enough length to make it bigger." Kathleen opened the clasp and caught the chains, then sat. "Now that we know it fits, let me find a good spell.

Trill sat again as Kathleen checked a handwritten table of contents. She flipped a few pages, scanned the words, and flipped back to the table of contents. She turned a number of pages, paused, and began to write. She flipped more pages and wrote again. She read what she'd written, crossed out and wrote more.

Kathleen tore the page off, checked the first page as she rewrote the lines. Then she tore off the sheet and wrote two more sheets. She handed one sheet to Shauna and one to Trill.

"I've written a combined hide and protect spell. It should prevent Art from finding the baby, but it also will protect Trill from being spelled again to control her."

That sounded perfect to her. She never wanted to be controlled to such an extent that she couldn't remember what she'd been doing.

Trill read through the spell and wondered if she would be able to contribute to its creation. She'd never done a spell before without using herbs and grasses, although she did have powerful ancestors.

Jason lifted his hands as if to hold back traffic. "Mom, you know I can't do this spell."

Trill frowned at Adam. She was afraid to ask why Jason couldn't do it.

Adam leaned close and whispered in her ear. "Jason's adopted. His father was more evil than mine."

Kathleen dropped the chains into the middle of the table, and spread it into a circle. "Fine. If anyone wants to help with the spell, hold part of the chain as we read the lines."

Kathleen and Reese were the first to touch the chain, followed by Shauna and Theron. Trill wrapped a couple of fingers around the chain and Adam gripped a portion beside her.

Abby rushed into the room followed by her brother. "Ooh, I want to help." She elbowed between Shauna and Jason and plopped into his lap.

Jason shifted her. "Hey, squirt."

"Hey, yourself. I'm taking your place." Abby added her hand to the chain.

Tony stretched between Kathleen and Trill. "I'll help." He wrapped his fingers around a section.

Trill couldn't believe all these people were willing to do this for her. Jamie hadn't touched the chain. For a second, Trill wondered if Jamie didn't want to help Adam in any way, but then it clicked. Jamie and Jason must be biological brother and sister with the same evil father.

"Let's begin on three," Kathleen said. "One, two, three…"

"We call forth the force of our ancestors to put your

protective power into this object we hold. May it hide the wearer and child from those who search for them and shield them from the influences of black magic."

A tingle passed through Trill's fingers. She hoped that meant the spell worked.

Abby released the chain. "I love when that happens." It must have zapped her, too.

Kathleen narrowed her eyes. "And when have you had cause to create a spell?"

Abby tried to jump off her brother's lap, but he held her in place.

"Yeah, squirt. You shouldn't be playing around with spells."

Abby stared down at her clasped hands. "I only use it to show me where I lost something or to help me speed-read an assignment."

Jason let his sister up.

Kathleen glared at her daughter. "We're talking later, young lady."

"Fine." Abby dropped into her own chair.

Kathleen picked up the chain, and held it out to Trill. "You should wear this under your clothes."

Trill took it and stood. "I'll put it on in the bathroom." It would be a good time to use the facilities anyway.

In the bathroom, Trill connected the chain in front and spun it around until the eagle hung down her tummy. Lucas' little foot or elbow rolled under the bird. She rubbed the sides of her belly. "Lucas, does that mean you like it?"

He moved again, but she didn't know what it meant. She returned to the dining room.

Theron stared at Adam with intensity. "—and then Art can get you."

Jamie whacked his chest with the back of her hand. "It wasn't his fault."

Theron wanted to abandon Adam out so he'd be caught. He didn't stand a chance if Art showed up with backup next time.

Trill stepped closer to the table and kept her eyes on the man she loved. If the others were going to be cruel to Adam, then she couldn't do as she'd promised. "I think we need to leave." Her gaze took in all the faces at the table. "Thanks for listening and all, but—"

Kathleen sprung from her chair. "No. You don't understand." She took Trill's arm. "We're trying to come up with a plan to draw Art out when we want him here, and not be taken by surprise."

Trill's tense muscles relaxed a bit, but she didn't like that Adam would be put at risk. He still believed his brother wouldn't hurt him, but she was sure that Art would do anything to finish his power spell, including kill Adam.

The older woman drew Trill back to her seat. "We're throwing out ideas now."

Jason leaned an elbow on the table, his other arm out of sight. The angle suggested he held his wife's hand in her lap. "Adam, what abilities does Art have?"

"He doesn't really have any, but when he casts a spell, it's very powerful. He's got the money to hire firepower, like the guys who attacked Trill and me in the woods."

Jason nodded. "Good to know." He skewered Trill with a stare. "What abilities do you two have?"

She glanced at Adam and he nodded. Might as well start with the strongest one. "I can freeze people with a touch."

Jason chuckled. "You mean like a real version of freeze tag?"

Adam grinned. "Not exactly. It's not like immobilizing someone. It's actually freezing. I thought I might end up with frostbite."

Theron glared at Adam. "And what did you do to her to

deserve that?"

Adam leaned forward. "I—"

Trill was incensed that Theron would assume that. "He didn't do anything. I misunderstood. I saw an email he got from his brother and jumped to the conclusion that they were working together." She glared at Theron. "I was angry and did it accidentally because I didn't know I could do it."

Adam gazed at her. She could freeze with a touch, but he could melt with that expression. "She used it effectively twice when we were attacked."

Jason cleared his throat.

Oops. She'd totally forgotten other people were there.

"Anything else, Trill?"

She shrugged. "I can change a person's emotions by having them recall an appropriate memory. That doesn't seem helpful for this."

"You never know." Jason's gaze switched to Adam. "What about you?"

"Is everybody sharing or just Trill and me?"

He came to these people for help. Trill didn't think he should be so arrogant.

Theron lifted his arm. "I can push and hit without touching."

He jammed his arm toward Adam and Adam huffed out a breath as his chair slid back an inch. He rubbed his chest.

Jason glared at his brother-in-law. "Cut it out."

Theron grinned and shrugged.

"Hey, you taught Jamie to fight so well. Can you teach me?" Trill couldn't believe Adam's question. That seemed to open himself up for a beating.

Theron smirked. "Sure. I can do that."

Jamie grabbed his face between her hands and turned it toward her. "You will not beat him up. He was a perfect gentleman."

Theron gripped her shoulders. "But, baby, he slept with you."

Trill couldn't hold back an audible indrawn breath. She knew they were imprisoned together, but hadn't thought of where they slept.

Jamie gave her a quick glance. "Theron, we slept in the same bed. He did not sleep *with* me. Get over it." She kissed him. "I love you."

Theron shoved his chair back, hauled his wife into his lap and buried his face in her hair. "Sorry. I went a little crazy that month you were missing."

"I can attest to that," Jason said. "Can we get back to planning?"

Jamie dropped an arm across the back of Theron's shoulders. "I can blast Art with lightning." She flexed her fingers. "Or burn him with my hands."

A chorus of male voices yelled, including Adam. "No!"

"But—"

Theron rubbed her belly. "Baby, you're due in less than two weeks. I don't want you anywhere near the action."

Jason glanced at his wife. "That goes for you, too."

Shauna put her hands on her hips. "But my levitation or protective bubbles might come in handy."

"We'll do without the levitation, and Mom can make protective bubbles, too. Your job is to protect you and our baby. Any sign of trouble, you put yourself into a protective bubble."

His gaze ran over the group. "I can make lightning, too, and I have infrared vision if we end up doing this in the dark."

Adam must have thought everyone was sharing enough. "I can throw fireballs."

"Mom can, too," Jason said.

"I can open locks with a wave of my hand," Adam said.

Jason rubbed his chin. "I don't see how that will be much use."

"I've got my premonitions. I've started doing them morning and night."

It seemed when Adam forced his premonitions, they only extended out about twelve hours. He hadn't realized it until the last time they were attacked. The visions that came without prompting could be hours or weeks away.

Kathleen waved her hand. "I can read surface thoughts." That was a weird way to say it.

Trill twisted toward Kathleen. "What are surface thoughts?"

"It's the top thought in someone's mind. I can't read memories, unless someone is thinking about them." She scanned the people around the table, and stopped at Theron. "Theron wishes that Adam had never come to town."

Theron's back thumped against the chair. "Hey. You could have guessed that."

Kathleen chuckled. "Yeah. You're really radiating it."

Trill couldn't blame him for his hostility. Adam had been a part of what happened to Jamie. "How far away can you read a mind?"

"I could easily pick up someone's thoughts in the driveway. Farther away if I know the person."

"I want to help," Tony said. "I can throw fireballs and make protective bubbles, too. We could have a multi-pronged attack."

Kathleen scowled at her son. "Tony, you're not participating."

"Mom, I'm not a kid. I'm old enough to legally drink."

Abby grabbed Tony's arm. "Good one. I'm old enough to legally smoke. I should help, too."

Kathleen shook her head. "And you better not be."

Abby fanned her hands. "That stuff stinks. Just saying

I'm old enough."

Reese hadn't volunteered an ability, so if he had any, they must not be useful in a battle.

Jason slapped the table, making Trill jump. "All right, people. Let's get back on mission."

That sounded very military. Trill hoped he had that kind of experience because they were going to need it. Art had paid men to help him and could do so again, and he was determined to the point of being delusional to finish his plan.

"First, let's figure out the best place for Adam and Trill to stay."

Jamie perked up. "They can stay with us."

Theron wrapped his arms around her. "No! I'm not risking you. Besides, Art knows who you are. If he sees you, there's no telling what he'll do."

"They'll stay here," Kathleen said.

Jason tapped the table with his fingertips. "Okay. Let's give you two a couple of days to get settled in and then Adam can take off the medicine bag. Maybe Trill can wear it for extra protection."

Adam nodded. Trill didn't want to agree to making Adam a target, but they weren't giving her a choice.

"While you're in the house, you're still hidden." He glanced at his mother. "Right, Mom?"

She nodded. "And your dad and I can reinforce the house protection, and enhance it with a hiding spell."

"Good. Adam, don't go out alone. Always take one of us guys with you. Since you can be tracked, don't go out with Trill. And Trill, you can visit Jamie or Shauna, but always go with me, Theron, Mom or Dad."

Jason was unbelievably bossy, but he seemed to know how to handle a mission. She never expected to be a mission, but she'd take that over being killed by an evil lunatic.

Trill's gaze traveled over all the eager faces. "Thanks so

much for helping us, especially with the history you have with Adam's family." Her gaze stopped on Kathleen. "And I can't thank you enough for letting us stay in your home."

Kathleen patted Trill's arm. "We've defeated evil before, and we won't let it win this time either."

For the first time since Adam rescued her from Art's spell, they had a chance. Not that Adam hadn't done well, but they would have had to run for maybe years, with the fear that the next time they were found, it would end with her and Lucas' deaths.

Adam settled a hand over her thigh. "Yeah, thanks everyone. I know I'm not a favorite person here, but I really appreciate what you're doing for Trill."

There was a chorus of well-wishing, and everybody stood.

"Abby, is your homework done?" Kathleen asked.

Abby rolled her eyes. "Yes, Mom. I did it when I got home."

Trill trailed behind the others with Adam as everyone headed into the foyer. Shauna and Jamie hugged Kathleen and each other before joining hands with their husbands and going out the door.

Trill stifled a yawn. It had been a long day, and a tense evening.

Kathleen touched her arm. "Why don't I show you where you'll sleep?"

"Thank you."

Trill followed Kathleen up the stairs and Adam trailed behind her. She stopped halfway between the first two doors on the left.

Kathleen waved at both. "You can use both or either. They were Jamie and Jason's rooms." She pointed to the end of the hall. "That's the bathroom, last door on the right. Good night." Kathleen continued down the hall and entered the room straight ahead, closing the door.

Adam grasped Trill's arms from behind, his warm breath in her ear. "What do you think? Separate or share?"

She spun, bumping her belly against him, and giggled. "Sometimes I still forget it's there." She wrapped her arms around his neck. She should probably tell him separate. They were guests in the people's home who were helping her, but she'd grown used to Adam sharing a bed with her, and so much more. She probably wouldn't be able to sleep without him.

She grinned. "There's less bedding to wash if we share."

He gave her a quick kiss. "Okay. You choose and I'll go get our bags."

One room was feminine and one masculine. She decided to choose the masculine one because it was farthest from Kathleen and Reese's room. And Adam wouldn't be sleeping in Jamie's bed again.

Footsteps came up the stairs. Adam stepped into the room, his bag over his shoulder and hers in his other hand. He set a package of fig Newton's on the dresser.

She funneled her fingers in his hair. "I love you."

He froze and she realized what she'd said. People said that so casually when someone did something nice for them, and she could have left it at that, but it was time to tell him.

She stared into his eyes. "I mean it. I really love you."

He beamed. That was the only way to describe his expression. "I'd pick you up and spin you around if little Lucas wasn't in the way. I love you." He buried his face in her hair. "I don't know what I'd do if anything happened to you or Lucas."

His love explained more than anything why he'd apologized and groveled to get her the protection she needed. That said as much or more than the battles he'd fought for her. Those encounters had been reaction. This had taken deliberate effort and perseverance, throwing himself on the mercy of the Ballards.

Chapter 13

Adam sat in the formal living room with Trill snuggled into his side, each reading a book they'd found in the Ballard's library. How many times had he and Jamie read in their separate chairs, hours on end, always an invisible wall between them? Trill's warmth seeped into him, giving him a contentment he'd never felt before, despite the danger still hovering over her.

He and Trill were sort of hiding out. Over the two days they'd been guests in the Ballard home, he noticed that no one used this room. Tony and Abby watched TV or played games in the family room, and Kathleen and Reese read or talked in the library.

Revealing his presence would start soon, but now there were more people who could protect Trill. He hoped it didn't take long before Art showed up. They needed to end this with Art far away from Trill, maybe sharing a cell with their father.

Trill tipped her head against his shoulder. "What time did Theron say he'd be here?"

"About four."

"Are you sure you want him to teach you Taekwondo? I'm afraid he's going to intentionally hurt you."

Adam was afraid it might happen, too. He kissed the top of her head. "I want to be more prepared the next time we see

Art. Theron taught Jamie to fight and she was amazing." He tipped her chin up, kissed her, and smiled. "If you give me a really sexy kiss before I go into battle with him, maybe he'll realize I don't want Jamie and will back off."

Theron had witnessed his breakdown when Jamie was rescued. He'd be as likely to tell Trill that Adam was unstable. Adam had told her most of the truth about his past, and she seemed to accept him. He hoped that didn't change.

Trill grinned, and rubbed the back of his neck. "Oh, yeah. I can do that."

Abby entered the front door and glanced into the living room. She dropped her backpack on the sofa and sat next to Trill. "Hi."

Adam and Trill greeted her. The last time he'd talk to an eighteen-year-old girl was when he was the same age.

Abby's gaze traveled from Trill's belly to each of their faces. "You two seem really serious about each other, but this is your brother's baby?"

Leave it to a kid to ask a question that an adult would find too delicate to ask.

Trill snuggled closer. "I was under Art's spell, so I don't remember anything about being with him. To me, it's like it didn't happen." She rubbed her belly. "Except for the baby."

Abby's gaze locked on him. "You're going to adopt him?"

Adam placed his hand over Trill's that still rested on the baby. "He's already mine. Trill's power forced out the evil spirit in the baby, and her grandmother asked their ancestors to give him a new one. Before the spirit entered the baby, he connected with me first. That's when Lucas became my son. Ours."

He stared into Trill's eyes. Hers held a sheen of tears. He hadn't told her how much the spirit's touch had affected him.

Abby's voice compelled him back to the present. "That's

so cool. I think that's what happened with Jason and Jamie because of my mom, except they were already born."

Trill squeezed Abby's arm. "Your mom has a wonderful, powerful spirit. I feel it every time she touches me."

The front door opened, and Abby glanced over her shoulder. Theron had come in. "I should go do my homework." She snatched up her backpack and headed toward the back of the house.

Theron stopped in front of them. He carried a large duffle bag. "Ready to spar?"

"Yes." Adam had put on sweats a short time before. He helped Trill up. In the foyer, he grabbed their coats from the closet.

Theron crossed his arms, bag at his feet. "You're not going to need yours. And you don't want to mess it up, anyway."

Adam's eyebrows rose. "We're doing this outside?" So much for a studio or gym.

"Of course." Theron smirked. "Be glad the snow melted, or I'd make you shovel a space for us to workout."

Theron led them into the kitchen and to the French doors on the far side, past the kitchen table where Adam and Trill had eaten breakfast the past two mornings.

Adam surveyed the backyard. At least the grass appeared thick. It would make a better landing than concrete. Because he would get thrown down.

Theron stood on the top step, his hand on the railing. "It's time to lose the medicine bag, so you can shine."

Adam extracted the bag from under his sweatshirt and lowered it over Trill's head. And so began the beacon for Art to find. The worry in her eyes killed him. "Remember your promise."

She frowned and then a grin lit her face. She stood on her toes, wrapping her arms around his neck, and bent over her belly. Sometimes she twisted a bit sideways so they could get closer. And closer made him forget where they were. Her warm lips and tongue made him want to go back inside with her. Her fingernails scraped up the back of his head sending shivers down his body. He may have moaned.

"Hey! We're supposed to be training." Theron's voice seemed to reach him through layers of cotton.

He stepped back. Trill's eyes twinkled. He grabbed a chair from the table for Trill and swung it around to face the yard, then took a couple deep, cold breaths, hoping it would cool his body.

He faced Theron and crossed his arms.

Theron tossed a head guard or protector—whatever it was called. He barely had time to untangle his arms and catch it so that it wouldn't smack him in the chest. He lowered it over his head and fumbled with buckling it. He hadn't worn one since high school gym class. "Where's yours?"

Theron chuckled. "I don't need one. I'm sparring with you."

Yeah, Adam wouldn't get fists or feet anywhere near Theron's head.

He followed Theron down the steps into the center of the yard.

Theron flung his arms out. "We'll start with stretches."

Adam followed along. He hit the gym regularly at home, but hadn't done any strenuous exercise since he'd been with Trill. It felt good to loosen up.

"Wait here." Theron jogged to the deck and removed equipment from his bag. He hurried back and handed Adam boxing gloves. "Put these on."

While Adam donned his gloves, Theron yanked on flat padded mitts, and lifted them to shoulder height. "Try to get past the mitts."

Adam punched over and over and Theron shifted a mitt

to catch each one. He gave Adam instructions to stiffen his wrists, use his shoulders, shift his feet this way and that. He kept up a monologue, and Adam tried to do as Theron instructed.

Theron had been right about not needing his coat. Sweat trickled down Adam's forehead, and he swiped at it with his forearm.

"Don't do that! It leaves you open. Next time wear a headband."

They continued for a few more minutes, and Adam grew more comfortable. He didn't make it through Theron's defenses, but there were a couple times that Adam hit the edge of a mitt.

Theron stepped back. "Stop. Now let's do kicks." He demonstrated how Adam should maneuver his feet and legs, naming two types of kicks.

The first few kicks were awkward and Theron yelled corrections. Adam had started to feel confident in his kicks when Theron called a halt.

"All right, gear off." Theron tossed his mitts toward the deck.

Adam did the same.

Theron crouched. "Now, I want you to use feet and hands. Anything to take me down."

That wasn't going to happen. He hadn't once gotten past Theron's mitts. No way, now that he was tired, would he touch Theron's body. He sucked in a breath and rolled his shoulders. He asked for this so he could protect Trill. He'd put his all into it.

Adam sent a punch toward Theron's jaw, but Theron caught him by the wrist, throwing him off balance. Theron deflected each kick or punch, calling out what Adam did wrong or how to correct it.

Adam punched at Theron's throat. Theron shifted right

and grabbed Adam's arm, propelling him into the air. Adam instinctively curled and hit the ground on his back with a grunt.

Theron stood over him and grinned. "That's it for today. You did better than I expected." He held out his hand. "I'll take the head guard."

Adam rolled to his side and unbuckled the guard, handing it over.

Theron stuffed it into his bag then added the rest of the gear. "I'll come back on Wednesday." He strode to a gate in the fence and left.

Trill padded down the stairs as Adam stood, and she wrapped her arms around him.

He held his arms out. "I'm all sweaty."

She rubbed her nose on his chest. "Just a stronger smelling Adam."

He laughed. "I need a shower." He dragged Trill's arms off him and dropped an arm around her shoulder.

As he opened the door, she glanced up. "Do you want help in the shower?" He loved that expression, the one she got just before they made love.

He kissed her nose. "I can't think of anything better than that."

***

Trill sat across the corner from Adam at the kitchen table. The day before, Kathleen had brought home a couple of apple pies from a bakery, and when Trill got hungry, it was the only thing she could think about. Maybe that's what a pregnant woman craving was. She cut off the point and scooped it into her mouth. She closed her eyes and tipped her head back. "Mmm. Are you sure you don't want a piece?"

He leaned back in the chair, his hands laced on his chest,

his legs stretched under the table. He shook his head. "No. I'm enjoying watching you eat."

She cut another piece and held the fork an inch from his mouth. "Have some."

"You eat it."

"If you don't take this, I'm going to turn my fork up-side down." She wouldn't, but he didn't know that.

He kept his gaze on her as his mouth surrounded the fork and slid the pie off it. He chewed and swallowed, then licked a crumb from his lips. Maybe she shouldn't have given it to him. He would be practicing with Theron soon, and now she wanted to kiss that spot he just licked and maybe more. If this was what he experienced watching her eat, no wonder he did it so intently.

She dragged in a breath and dropped her gaze to the plate. No. Pie craving paled next to Adam craving. Sometimes, it seemed as if they'd still be together after the Art scariness was taken care of, especially when Adam said the baby was his. But he'd never actually said anything about having a permanent relationship. They'd known each other such a short time, and been thrown together practically every hour from the first. She wouldn't blame him if he needed time apart.

She took another bite and another.

Theron entered the kitchen. "Hey, we're going to the dojo. I figured you should see some real sparring. Then we can practice."

Trill shoveled the last bite into her mouth. "Can I come watch?"

Theron tipped his head. "You two aren't supposed to go out together."

She stood. "But Adam only took the medicine bag off yesterday. Art can't have tracked him here already."

Theron appeared ready to tell her no.

Maybe a little more pressure. "I thought you were the big, bad Taekwondo guy. You don't think you can protect me?"

He sighed. "Fine. You can come."

She grinned. "Thanks." In a rush, she rinsed her plate and glass and put them in the dishwasher.

By the time she'd gotten to the foyer, Adam had her coat out. He helped her into it and they left in Theron's SUV.

Adam had insisted she sit in front since it would be easier to get in and out.

It had a new car smell and was extremely clean. "New car?"

Theron blushed.

She almost laughed. "You seem uncomfortable. Green guilt?"

"No. My old car died a couple months ago coming home from campus and Jamie had to come get me. We had my car towed to the mechanic and I had to drive Jamie's car. A few days later, this was sitting in our driveway when I got home, with a big bow on the windshield. Jamie insisted that I needed a reliable car in case she went into labor when I wasn't with her." He glanced at Trill. "She bought it with her inheritance."

That made him seem more human, and old fashioned. Guilt over his wife providing for him. It was sweet that he didn't feel as if he was entitled to it.

Theron turned into a parking lot and found an empty space in front of *Shotokan Studio*. A smaller bag than he'd had the other day was in his hand. He pointed to the closer of the two large red mats. "We're sparring there." He glanced at Trill's belly. "I'll see if Joe can bring a chair out for you."

He was gone before she could say he didn't need to, but it would be better for her feet if she didn't have to stand for more than fifteen minutes. With a pregnant wife, Theron had to know that.

Adam kept his arm around her as they waited. A class of kids in Karate outfits, probably around ten-years-old, practiced different poses and kicks.

She jumped when they yelled.

Theron glanced at the kids and then to Adam. "Have you been in one of these places before?"

"No, I haven't. It's nothing like the gym I use."

A man with military short blond hair crossed to the center of their mat and started punching and kicking the air. He was a similar size to Theron. He must be Theron's opponent.

Something rolled behind Trill, and she glanced over her shoulder.

An older man rolled an office chair across the floor. "Here you go, young lady." He stopped the chair beside her. "I'm Joe."

They introduced themselves.

Joe shook Adam's hand. "Theron says he's putting you through a crash course."

"Hopefully, with the one-on-one I pick it up quickly."

"Theron's one of our best teachers. If anyone can do it, he can."

Besides teaching Jamie, and now Adam, Theron taught others. And if Joe thought he was a great teacher, there must be more to Theron than she'd seen so far.

Trill expected Joe to leave, but he stayed beside her. "You're in for a treat."

She sat and Adam stood behind her with his hands on her shoulders. His thumbs made circles at the base of her neck, and she wondered if he realized that he did it, hoping he wouldn't stop for a while.

Theron must have been in a locker room since he now wore a Karate outfit. He stopped on the mat in front of the guy who'd been warming up. "Hey, Eric."

They talked for a minute and backed away from each other. Most of the adults and kids who'd been in classes or working on their own circled the mat, the younger ones sitting on the floor. They must have known this would be an exciting show.

A whistle blew and they started bouncing on the balls of their feet. Theron kicked out, and Eric countered. Eric punched and Theron brushed the arm away as if it was nothing. Then the action sped up as if someone had turned on a video at double-speed. Smacks of flesh on flesh, and grunts echoed in the room. Yells, kicks and spins made her dizzy. They flowed with such speed, it was hard to keep track of Theron.

Adam's hands tightened on her shoulders. "I can't imagine ever being able to do that."

Trill covered his hand with hers.

Eric dropped, but bounced back up. Did that even count as some kind of loss? She couldn't believe how quiet the large group of people had become. Theron and Eric were breathing hard as they circled each other, and struck out again.

The whistle blew, and they instantly stopped, backed away from each other, and bowed. The crowd broke out into applause and cheers. Trill stood and clapped.

Adam stepped beside her and whispered in her ear. "I can't believe he agreed to teach me. It was like watching a martial arts movie."

The crowd dispersed as Theron headed to a bubbler, and gulped down two cups of water. He squashed the cup and dropped it in the trash, then came over to Adam and Trill. "Ready to workout?"

Adam held Trill closer. "I knew you had to be good since Jamie's an awesome fighter, but I didn't expect that level of expertise."

Theron shrugged one shoulder. "You get out of it what you put into it."

There was more to it than that, but it made Trill like Theron a bit more, since he didn't let his skill go to his head.

Adam pointed to the mat Theron had used. "Are we practicing here?"

"Yeah." Theron headed to the center of it.

Adam led Trill back to the chair and she sat. Since no one else watched this match, she felt a bit conspicuous being the only person in the room sitting on a chair.

Theron ran them through the same warm-ups as before. Both put on head protection this time, then Adam did kicks and hits, but for a shorter time with few corrections. Theron demonstrated a double-kick and had Adam repeat it until Theron seemed satisfied. Theron showed Adam how to block various attacks, then demonstrated in slow motion for Adam to get the form right. He gradually sped up.

Adam glanced at her and didn't block a kick, toppling flat onto his back. He rolled and as he shoved up, Theron knocked him over with a slow kick.

"Now, get up," Theron yelled. "Never take your eyes off your opponent, no matter how pretty the distraction."

It made Trill feel almost guilty since she was the distraction.

Adam scrambled to his feet and got into position. Theron threw faster punches, but nowhere near as fast as with his previous opponent. Adam kept up, and gave an occasional punch or kick, always blocked by Theron.

Finally, Theron called a halt, and clapped Adam on the shoulder. "You did great. Now, let's get you two back to the Ballard's."

Back at the house, Theron led them to the door and unlocked it. "Practice morning and afternoon tomorrow, and the following morning. I'll come by and work with you day after tomorrow about four." He left them in the doorway.

Adam had progressed in this new fighting skill, but not enough to overcome Art's bulk. Each time trouble found them, their combined talents and luck had saved them. Trill hoped luck hadn't run out.

Chapter 14

It had been a week since Trill had gone to the Martial Arts studio and the Ballard house had begun to feel more like a prison than a safe house. All the other places they'd hidden, they'd done fun activities, but now, since Adam had stopped wearing the protective medicine bag, he'd gone out without her. They couldn't chance that Art would find them together.

The only things she'd done since they'd arrived in Rawlins were read, watch Adam practice Taekwondo or cook dinner. When she'd asked if she could vacuum, she'd been informed that the housekeeper took care of that when she came in twice a week.

Trill had been excited when Jamie invited her over for a girls' day. Before leaving the house, Kathleen informed her that Jamie's house had the same protection spell as hers, so she'd have that extra invisibility power on her visit. Kathleen parked in the driveway at Jamie's house beside another car.

The two women got out of the car and when they were halfway up the walk, the front door opened. Jamie grinned. "Mom, Trill, come on in. Shauna got here a few minutes ago."

Kathleen stayed by the door. "I'll leave you girls to chat for a couple hours while I put through orders at *Mystical Moment*."

Trill raised a brow. "What's *Mystical Moment*?"

Jamie grinned. "It's the store Mom and Dad own. It has all kinds of—" she wiggled her fingers "—witchcraft stuff."

"They've got herbs and tinctures?" Not everybody had the option to harvest their own herbs like Gram did.

Jamie nodded. "Yeah, and black and white candles, and black robes, and magic wands."

"Magic wands?"

"They're not real. They're for fun." Jamie rubbed her tummy. "I'm going to get one for my little girl."

Kathleen grabbed the doorknob. "How about if I return with lunch?"

Shauna sauntered into the entry area. "Oh, yeah. I'm craving pizza."

Jamie bumped Shauna's shoulder. "It's too early for you to have cravings."

Shauna stuck her fist on her hip and glared at her sister-in-law. "Hey, it's my craving and I want pizza."

Smoothing ruffled feathers seemed to be Kathleen's specialty. "Pizza okay for all of you?"

These people were kind enough to feed her, Trill didn't care what she ate. "Fine by me."

"Me, too," Jamie said. A tea kettle whistled. "Thanks. See you later, Mom." Jamie waddled away, and the other two women followed.

In the kitchen, Jamie turned off the burner under the steaming kettle. "I've got all kinds of tea."

Shauna opened a cupboard with at least twenty boxes of tea, and they each selected a different kind and prepared their cups.

Jamie uncovered a plate of scones and took it to the kitchen table, setting it next to pots of strawberry and peach jam, and a butter dish. She distributed knives and small plates. "How are you doing?"

Trill rubbed the sides of her belly. "I'm okay. Starting to

feel trapped."

Jamie grimaced. "Try that for a month behind locked doors. At least, you can go outside if you really want to."

Trill squeezed Jamie's hand. "Sorry. I go out on the back deck to watch Adam practice. I have nothing to complain about."

"Yeah, nothing except a crazed psycho who wants to kill you." Jamie took a scone and buttered it.

Trill shivered. "Yeah, that."

Shauna slathered strawberry jam on a scone. "Jason said Adam is growing on him." Her gaze met Trill's. "Adam really cares about you."

Jamie set her cup down. "Theron's calmed down about me being around Adam now that he's seen the way he cares for you."

Heat bloomed in Trill's cheeks. "Uh, yeah. Theron arrived once while we were, um, kissing." Adam's hands had been under her shirt, and both of them were breathing hard, obviously not a simple kiss. In Adam's arms, she was safe and loved, and forgot everything else, even that Theron would be arriving any minute.

Shauna licked jam off her lip. "Jamie, you make the best scones."

"It's Mom's recipe."

Shauna laughed. "She gave the recipe to me, too, but when I made them, they turned out horrible. Jason took one bite and pitched them into the backyard for the birds."

Jamie giggled. "Try it again. Where is Jason taking Adam today?"

This was the third time Jason took Adam out so Art's searches had a chance to find him. While in the Ballard home Adam was untraceable by any spell Art might use. They'd gotten groceries once, and worked out at the dojo.

"To lunch," Shauna said. "Since we're having lunch

here, he figured they'd eat out."

Jason had picked Adam up shortly before she and Kathleen left. They would drive around until lunch time.

Trill cut into her second scone. She shouldn't eat another one, but they were delicious. She hoped it wouldn't spoil her lunch. The last time Trill had gotten together with other women for girl talk had been before Art. These women treated her as if she belonged there, and she hadn't had that since living on the reservation.

The scone on Jamie's plate was barely nibbled. She sipped her tea. At nearly full-term, Jamie's stomach was probably miniscule. "Trill, what are you going to do after Art's taken care of?"

Trill took her time spreading jam. "We haven't discussed what happens after. Adam says he loves me. Us."

"He looks at you like he can't get enough of you," Jamie said. "He's not here just because he wants to protect you."

"I agree," Shauna said. "He can't keep his hands off you. And, only a man in love would bring you here and beg for our help."

He'd told her he loved her after she'd said it first, and he'd put himself between her and Art time after time. She blinked back tears. "Thank you."

Jamie stood. "Why don't we go into the living room?" She doubled over and slammed her elbows onto the table, her hands clenched into fists. Her eyes squeezed shut as she huffed repeatedly.

Shauna jumped up and put her arm around Jamie. "Are you okay?"

Jamie lifted a finger, still huffing.

That was a part of pregnancy Trill wasn't looking forward to. She'd been so focused on staying alive, she hadn't thought about what was to come later in her pregnancy.

After a few more seconds, she stood. "Either that was a really strong Braxton-Hicks or I'm in labor. What's the time?"

Shauna glanced at her phone. "Ten-twenty."

"Okay, let's say ten-nineteen." Jamie sat back down.

Trill imagined she'd be going crazy when she realized she was in labor. "How come you're so calm?"

"Theron and I had birthing classes. They told us all kinds of stuff. Like, with a first birth, I'll probably go twenty or thirty minutes before the next pain. It could be hours before I'm ready to go to the hospital."

"When do you take those classes?" Trill wouldn't mind knowing what to expect.

"We started ours at seven months."

"Wow. That's less than a month away for me. It's still weird that in my head I've only been pregnant a month."

Jamie chuckled. "I wish I could have slept through the throwing up stage."

Shauna crossed her arms on the table. "I haven't been nauseous yet. I hope it stays away."

Jamie leaned forward, put her hands on her belly and started huffing, not as evenly as the previous time. Her contorted expression suggested the pain was worse this time. In a few months, it would be Trill's turn.

Trill glanced at Shauna. "How long?"

"Eight minutes!" Shauna rubbed Jamie's back. "Jamie, you said thirty minutes."

A couple more huffs, then Jamie took a deep breath and tipped her head back. "Either I peed myself or my water just broke."

Shauna grabbed her arm. "This is way too fast."

"It doesn't matter. It's happening. I better call my doctor."

Shauna retrieved the phone from the kitchen counter and

handed it to Jamie.

Jamie scrolled through her phone and put it to her ear, as Shauna paced behind her. "This is Jamie Jarvis. I've had two labor pains, eight minutes apart and my water broke on the second one."

She nodded. "Yes. Dr. Bradshaw."

She stared past Trill's shoulder. "All right. We'll leave right away."

She set the phone down and doubled over, huffing.

"How long?" Trill asked.

Shauna glanced at her phone. "Seven minutes."

Jamie took a deep breath.

Shauna touched her shoulder. "Do you have a bag packed?"

"Yeah. It's the red one in my closet."

"I'll go get it. Trill, get our coats and shoes. Jamie, call Theron."

Having something to do calmed Trill's nerves. She hadn't expected to experience this part of pregnancy until it was her time. She hoped she would handle it as well as Jamie did. Beside the front door, Trill collected shoes and coats, and brought them to the kitchen then grabbed a trash bag and a couple kitchen towels for Jamie to sit on in the car.

Coming to Jamie's house, Trill hadn't been concerned about Art. He would likely not have been able to find her, and if he had, Kathleen would have helped her fight him. Now, if he found her in route to the hospital, she and Shauna would have to protect Jamie.

Shauna rushed in with the red bag, and they slipped on their shoes and coats. Jamie had another contraction at the door.

Shauna yelled out. "Under seven minutes. Jamie, is it Hastings Memorial Hospital?"

"Yes."

Shauna wrapped an arm around Jamie. "Okay, let's go."

Shauna beeped the car locks and Trill rushed to the far side, opened the back door and spread the bag and towels where Jamie would sit behind the driver. Shauna helped Jamie inside, and she settled into her seat.

Shauna screamed, and Trill glanced up. Art had flung Shauna away from the car, and with her keys in his hand, he climbed into the front seat, and started the engine.

Trill wouldn't get out of the car unless Jamie did, but the poor woman was having another contraction. Trill had no idea how many minutes since the last.

Jamie's phone! Trill dove into Jamie's purse on the floor and plucked out the phone. She kept it low as she scrolled to the last call made. Theron. She hit call, and waited a few seconds. "Art. Let Jamie go. I'm the one you want. You don't need her." She hoped Theron could hear her.

The tires squealed as he reversed out of the driveway and again after he shifted into drive. "She's the reason my father's in prison. She comes with us."

He was driving too fast for them to jump out now without killing them.

Trill's anger mounted. "Your father's in prison because he kidnapped Jamie and killed people."

If Trill hadn't been with Jamie, she'd have been safe from Art. Trill deserved whatever Art did to her if Jamie or her baby died. Jamie must be reliving the first time she'd been kidnapped. Trill wished they hadn't come to the Ballards for help.

Trill could try to freeze Art, but then he'd crash, and what would happen to them? She was too big to squeeze between the front seats to steer the car.

Jamie gasped and started huffing. That must have been less than eight minutes. Soon she'd be incapacitated, and even more at Art's mercy.

Maybe Trill could use her freeze skill for something else. She held up her hand, wiggled her fingers, and whispered. "Jamie, do you remember my ability?"

Jamie gave a slow nod.

"I think I can numb the contractions. Do you trust me to try?"

She nodded again.

Jamie didn't have much of a choice, but Trill had to work on trusting herself. She'd used the ability three times and it had gone deep. Now, she had to concentrate it to only an inch or so. She called up hatred for Art and cold invaded her hand.

Jamie stopped huffing. "Start at the top."

"Okay." Trill tapped her fingertips close to Jamie's breasts. Maybe that wasn't deep enough. She held them a second and slid beside that spot. She worked in rows, back and forth, touch, move over, touch.

Jamie's shoulders dropped. "It's working. What you've covered isn't contracting anymore, but below it is." One thing was going in their favor.

Art slammed his hand on the steering wheel. "Shut up back there!"

Trill finished the numbing and whispered. "I don't know how long it will last." She eased a bit away from Jamie and glared at Art. "How did you find me?"

He met her gaze in the mirror. "I tracked my brother down yesterday and followed him back to that huge house. I came back this morning and watched him leave with that guy again. I circled the house, trying to find a way in, but by the time I got back to the front, you and that older lady were driving away. I jumped in my car and followed you."

If Jamie hadn't gone into labor, they would have been safe inside the house, but Trill couldn't blame Jamie for their capture.

They and their babies might not survive the day.

***

Adam grabbed the door handle. Jason had pulled into a parking space at the *Cozy Corner Diner.*

Jason's phone rang, and he yanked it out. "It's Shauna." He swiped and held the phone to his ear. "Hi, honey." His face paled. "No!"

What was bad for Jason was bad for Adam. He waited, his hands balled into fists.

"Your car? Thank God." He paused. "I—um—have a tracker on your car." Shauna's voice grew louder. "We'll discuss it later. Right now, it might save Jamie and Trill's lives. I gotta go."

Jason disconnected the call and blew out a long breath. "Art has Jamie and Trill in Shauna's car. Let me call Theron, and then I'll start tracking them."

He put the phone back to his ear. "Theron—" A pause. "Say that again."

He tapped his phone and Theron's voice filled the car. "Jamie called. Art has Jamie and Trill. Trill tried to talk him into letting Jamie go, but he blames her for his father being in prison."

Leave it to his brother and his twisted ideas.

Theron's anguished voice snapped him back. "Jamie's in labor."

Jason's voice cracked. "Theron, we'll get her back."

"And it better not take a month this time." Anger tinged Theron's voice.

"As soon as we hang up, I'll start tracking Shauna's car."

"And I'll track Jamie's phone. Meet you there. Wherever that is."

The call ended and Jason tapped and tapped his phone.

"Got it. They're moving north out of town." He set his phone into a holder.

"I'm sorry I got you involved in our problems. I never expected Jamie to be caught up with my family again." Adam cared about Jamie. He blamed himself for drawing Art to Rawlins and Jamie.

Jason took a fast turn. "We're getting them back."

Adam sucked in a breath. "It's my fault. Trill was so excited this morning about the girls' day, I totally forgot to do a premonition. We could have set Art up without putting the girls in danger." These people had befriended him, were risking themselves for Trill, and he'd let them careen into a life threatening situation that he could have prevented.

"I'm going to do a premonition." He closed his eyes and concentrated on Trill. An image of a car sitting in tall grass came to him. A house with an askew railing was a few feet away. The vision couldn't be more than a few minutes ahead of the actual event.

"They're in the backyard of an abandoned house. Art is holding a gun on the girls and telling them to get out of the car. He has Trill zip tie Jamie's hands behind her back. Now he's checking she did it, then zip ties Trills hands in front. The house door is broken and he takes them inside.

"They're walking through the kitchen and into the living room. Oh, God. There's a table with symbols written on it already. Art made Jamie sit against a wall and has Trill zip tie her ankles, then he forces Trill to get on the table and clips her zip tie over her head."

Adam opened his eyes and stared out the window. "I can't watch anymore. I've seen Trill die three times."

"We're almost there." Jason slowed.

Adam pointed. "That's the house." It was the same yellow as the premonition. If it was a premonition. It could have been in real time and Trill was dying at this moment.

Jason parked in front of the next house and they got out.

Theron skidded to a stop behind them.

Jason grabbed Theron's arm. "You made great time."

"Yeah. I had good incentive. What's the plan?" Theron held his arms rigidly out from his sides, and flexed his fingers.

Jason pointed at the largest window, high up since the house was a split level. "Adam says they're in the living room." He glanced down at Theron's fists. "Can you do that punch thing through glass?"

"I've never tried. Maybe it'll bounce off the glass and punch me instead."

Jason squinted. "We can sneak in the back."

Adam shook his head. "The door squeaks."

Jason pulled out his gun. "Okay. Adam, you're going to boost me to the window, and I'll wing Art. Theron, you get to the back door and fly in as soon as you hear the shot."

If Adam had the gun, he'd shoot Art dead. Up to this point, he probably couldn't do it, but now that Art possessed the woman Adam loved, he would do anything to protect her. Even kill his own brother. He'd never held a gun before, but he'd keep shooting until all the bullets were gone. Then he'd never have to worry about Trill again.

They crept together up to the house, then Theron disappeared around the left side. The top of Jason's head was an inch below the window. Adam hoped he'd give Jason enough height. He straightened his arms and laced his fingers together between his knees and squatted a bit.

Jason planted his foot, grabbed the window sill with his free hand and lifted his other foot. Adam straightened his legs, but couldn't give anymore height. Jason was heavy with muscle and Adam was afraid his arms would slip at the critical time.

Jason lifted his gun hand, and Adam leaned against the

wall, stiffening his body, not wanting to mess up Jason's aim. Seconds ticked by.

Maybe Art was already plucking Lucas from Trill's body. He prayed she was still alive. A battle raged inside of him. Adam wanted to be the one to rescue Trill, but he'd brought Trill to these people because he couldn't do it on his own. He wished he was beside Jason, staring into the room. It might already be too late.

The explosion above Adam's head startled him. The gunshot was louder than he expected. He let out a breath.

"Down!" Jason yelled.

Adam opened his hands and Jason hit the ground and ran in the direction Theron had gone. Adam raced to the front door and held his hand over the lock. He had no idea what he'd find inside. The lock clicked. He threw open the door and entered, racing up the short flight of stairs.

Jamie lay, writhing on the floor, one arm over her head, the other protecting her belly. Theron dashed across the room. "Jamie!" He punched out his arm, hand fisted, and Art flew against the wall, his bloody left shoulder leaving a stain on the paint. Theron knelt beside his wife and gathered her into his arms. "Baby, are you okay?"

Adam sprinted to Trill and unclipped the zip tie from a hook.

"No!" Art lunged, knife raised. "You're not taking my power."

Adam's heart pounded as he swept Trill off the table. He stumbled on debris and dropped to his knees. Two shots rang out as the knife imbedded into the table, right where Trill was a moment ago. Art followed the knife down, hit the table then slid to the floor.

Adam sunk down, Trill clutched in his lap.

On the other side of the table, his brother lay in his own blood. "They were mine."

Adam tightened his arms around Trill. "They're mine and I'm theirs."

Art's eyes closed for the last time.

Adam kissed Trill's forehead. Tears streaked her cheeks, and his, too. He didn't care if anyone saw. "You're safe now. He can't hurt you anymore." He glanced at the other men. "Anyone have a knife?"

Jason squatted beside him, an open knife in his hand and sliced through the tie binding Trill's wrists.

Jamie's voice was exasperated. "I tried to compel him and nothing happened except I got a headache. Then I melted the zip ties and burnt him, but he kneed me in the head." She struggled, enclosed in Theron's arms.

"Baby—"

Jason dropped a hand on her shoulder. "Jamie, you did great distracting Art, but he might have turned that knife on you." He glanced at Theron. "Your husband wouldn't have forgiven me if you'd been hurt."

Jason helped Jamie up.

Trill scrambled off Adam's lap and he jumped up, giving her a hand. She hugged Jamie. "I'm so sorry I put you through this."

If it wasn't such a serious situation, Adam would laugh at the sight of two pregnant women hugging.

Trill stepped back and into his arms, exactly where he needed her.

Theron frowned at his wife. "I thought you were in labor?"

"Trill numbed the muscles and stopped it, but—" she rubbed her belly "—I had a contraction a couple minutes ago."

It had been painful when Trill froze him, and hard to breathe. "Was that safe?"

Trill kept her gaze on Jamie. "I was careful to not numb

deep. I thought it was safer than Jamie having the baby with Art there."

Jamie continued to rub her belly. "The baby moved around the whole time."

Theron studied Jamie. "Why don't I get you to the hospital?" He scanned the other faces. "Is that all right with everybody? You can finish up here?"

Jason clamped a hand on Theron's shoulder. "Go. Take care of my sister."

Theron and Jamie headed toward the front door. "You wait on the front steps while I get the car. It's parked down the road."

"No. I can go with you." She doubled over and huffed in and out. "Okay. I'll wait."

Theron rubbed her back, and when she straightened up, they finished leaving the house. Moments later, Theron raced down the driveway.

Jason pulled out his phone. "I'll call the police."

As much as possible, Adam had tried to stay between Trill and Art's body, but at the moment, she had a clear view. "Can I wait outside, too?"

"I'll wait with you." He led her out of the nightmare.

Chapter 15

Trill curled up next to Adam in bed, only now beginning to feel warm. The Ballard family had rushed to the hospital to welcome the newest family member, leaving Trill and Adam alone in the house.

Adam rubbed her arm. “Before the police arrived, you said you had something to tell me in private.”

She nodded. “Art…” Just saying that cold-hearted man’s name sent chills through her.

Adam snuggled her closer. “What about him?”

“H-he said that when I disappeared he found another girl and impregnated her.”

He stiffened. “Where is she? She could starve to death if no one’s taking care of her.”

Like she could have. If Art had stopped delivering food, would she have wasted away when it was gone? No. Mazy would have checked up on her before that. She hoped.

“At his house. He said he didn’t have to spell her.”

“I can’t imagine any woman wanting to be with him.”

She grabbed his hand. “He said, since he found me again, he could kill her.” They’d saved two more lives without realizing it. She didn’t know how two brothers could be more different.

“Did he say what her name was?”

“No.” It probably didn’t matter to Art. The woman was

just a vessel for power.

"I'm going to make sure that baby gets Art's estate." He gazed down at her. "Unless you want part of it?"

She shuddered. "No! I don't want anything from him."

He smiled. "I didn't think so, but thought I should ask. We'll leave tomorrow, and visit this woman the day after that."

"You want me to go with you?"

He squinted. "Well, of course. Why wouldn't I?"

A tear slid down her cheek. "After all the trouble I put you through, I didn't know if you wanted to be with me anymore."

Adam tipped her chin up, rubbed a thumb across her cheek, and frowned. "Why would you think that? You know I love you. More than I ever thought I could love anyone."

She blinked to clear her vision. "I love you, too."

He kissed her. "Don't ever doubt that. I know it's kind of crazy twisted, but if not for Art, I never would have met you."

She looped her arm around his neck. "I never thought of it like that. All that bad stuff had to happen for us to find each other and fall in love."

He hugged her tight. "I don't know about all of it. If I'd done a better job of protecting you, you wouldn't have almost died."

"But I didn't." Trill stared into his eyes. "Tell me a premonition."

"Okay." He closed his eyes, and the corners of his lips turned up. "I see you and me, holding hands, standing in front of a man with an open book in his hands. Your Gram and Wolf are looking on with smiles on their faces." He opened his eyes and grinned.

She narrowed her eyes. "That can't happen today. We're not seeing my family." She poked him in the chest. "You're lying."

Adam grabbed her hand. "No. It wasn't a premonition. Marry me, Trill. Make it true. We're a family already, so let's make it official."

She studied his warm, hopeful eyes. "Yes. I want that, too."

His arm tightened around her, and he kissed her. "I'll have to tell you I love you every day so you don't doubt me."

"Can you show me, too?"

He grinned. "I can do both. I'm great at multitasking."

***

Trill put down her fork, and leaned back in the chair in Adam's kitchen. She'd eaten half of her second chocolate chip pancake and all three pieces of bacon. Adam was a wonderful cook, well, at least what she'd had of the simple meals he'd prepared. She'd like to make some meals with him again, like they'd done in the RV.

Doing it in this kitchen would be easier. The home that used to belong to Adam's grandparents had an impressive kitchen. Granite countertops, a six burner gas range with two ovens, and more dishes than she knew what to do with.

The refrigerator was nearly empty when they opened it to put in the food they'd purchased. She'd questioned him, not imagining him usually having an empty refrigerator, knowing he hadn't taken the time to empty it when they left Boston so quickly. He admitted to having a housekeeper come in weekly.

"Is this where we'll live?"

He scanned the room. "I'm not sure. I've toyed with selling it, but I spent so much time here growing up."

"It's a beautiful house."

He sighed. "But it's not really a home. I want our kids to

have a huge backyard with play equipment. I want them to be able to walk to a friend's house. When I stayed here with my grandparents, their driver took me to visit friends because it wasn't safe for a kid to walk."

She found the house a bit overwhelming. "If you sold it, you could buy a really comfortable house in Rawlins and have money left over."

His eyes widened. "Rawlins? You want to live in Rawlins?"

"It's a nice town. And I really like Jamie and Shauna and Kathleen. I got really close, like I'd known them for years."

He rubbed his chin as if he was thinking, but his eyes twinkled. "Maybe I should give Theron a call to make sure he wouldn't mind if I move to town."

She nudged his knee with her foot. "Come on. He got over it already."

"All right. We'll call a realtor after we talk to the pregnant girl."

She squealed, and couldn't believe a squeal had actually come out of her. Adam pushed his chair back and before he could stand, she dropped into his lap. "Thank you." She kissed him.

He wrapped his arms around her, and nuzzled her neck, his love surrounding her. She'd never expected to find anyone like Adam, a man who demonstrated his love for her by making sacrifices for her, putting her welfare ahead of everything. "What else can I do to make you react like this?"

"Just keep loving me."

"That's easy." He tapped her back. "Let's go see that girl."

They got their coats on and headed out the front door. Trill's car was still in the garage, so Adam had parked on the street. They got into his car and he drove the short distance to Art's house.

Trill stared at the house. It wasn't as large as Adam's, but was still large, made of huge, yellow stones. It emanated a sense of menace, probably from a spell. She'd never approach this house alone. She grabbed Adam's hand. "Are you okay going into Art's house?"

He squinted. "What do you mean?"

"He was your brother and he died yesterday."

He took her hand. "He died trying to kill you. There's no love left for him."

She could understand that. If Art had given up on trying to take her, Adam wouldn't have wished his brother harm.

Now they were here, she wasn't sure what they'd say to the woman.

Adam opened her door. "It's all right. We're going to figure out how to take care of her."

She put her hand in his, and he helped her up. She kissed him. "I love you." Her heart burst at being able to telling him that.

"I don't deserve you, but I'm keeping you anyway." They walked up to the door, and Adam rang the doorbell. Beethoven's Fifth played.

She giggled. "Seriously? That so doesn't seem like your brother." And then she remembered Art was dead and wished she could take it back.

Adam squeezed her hand. He must have noticed a change in her expression.

The door opened and a five foot tall girl who appeared no older than Abby squinted at them. "Can I help you?"

Trill had no expectations of what the woman would be like, but seeing this tiny girl threw her. She glanced at Adam.

"I'm Art's brother, Adam."

The girl tipped her head. "Okaay. Art never told me he had a brother."

He fished out his wallet and showed her his driver's

license. "We aren't close."

"You don't look much alike."

"I resemble our mother, and he took after our father."

She glanced at Trill's swollen belly and stepped back. "Come on in."

Adam led the way to the living room, maybe to let the girl know he'd been in the house. He sat on the couch, Trill sat beside him, and the girl settled in the closest chair.

"I'm Trill Song, Adam's fiancée." It was the first time she'd said it and it thrilled her.

"That's a beautiful name. I'm Bryanna Rochelle."

Adam slid forward. "Bryanna, Art died in an altercation day before yesterday."

They'd decided not to give the girl details unless they had to.

She covered her mouth and tears sprang to her eyes. "No. I know he didn't always treat people right, but…"

Adam squatted on the floor in front of her and took her hand. "Bryanna, is there someone you can call to stay with you?"

She shook her head. "My mom died a few months ago. I lost track of my friends. Art was all I had."

"How did you and Art meet?" Trill asked.

"After Mom died, I couldn't pay the rent for our apartment. I was homeless. Art volunteered at the shelter I was staying in."

Trill exchanged surprised expressions with Adam. No way would Art volunteer for anything.

Bryanna stared at her twisting hands. "He said our mothers had been friends."

Adam stiffened. "Pam Rochelle?"

"You remember her?"

Adam nodded. "You were…three or four the last time I saw you. How old are you now?"

"Twenty."

Trill hoped it eased Bryanna a little to find a connection with Adam. She hated the pain her next question would cause the girl, but she needed to know. "Bryanna, how did your mother die?"

"She was run down by a hit-and-run driver. They didn't find who did it."

Trill had an idea who'd done it. In the dictionary, Art's name would be the description for despicable bastard.

Trill hated to probe, but they needed to know for sure. "Art told me you were having his baby."

Bryanna covered her mouth and nodded. "And now my baby doesn't have a daddy."

No. Now, the baby would be born and the mother would live.

Adam rubbed Bryanna's hand. "This baby is Art's only descendant. I'm going to make sure you receive his estate so that you won't be homeless again."

"Thank you. I don't know how I'm going to take care of a baby. And this big house…"

Adam glanced at Trill and raised an eyebrow. "Trill and I are selling my house and moving to the western part of the state to a small, friendly town called Rawlins. You could sell this and find a smaller house out there, too." He waved a hand toward Trill. "The cousins could grow up near each other."

Bryanna bit her lip. "You'd help me do that?"

Trill struggled to her feet. "Of course, we will."

The others stood and Trill gave Bryanna an awkward hug. She placed her hand over Bryanna's flat tummy. "And by the time this little one is born, I'll have somewhat figured out parenting and can help you."

"Thank you, both." Tears streaked her cheeks. "I don't know what I would have done."

They exchanged phone numbers and Adam gripped Bryanna's hand. "We'll call you in a couple days."

They got in Adam's car, and Trill leaned over and kissed him. "You were so wonderful to offer to help Bryanna."

"I had to. Once she comes into this money, I don't want someone like Art to take advantage of her and leave her and my niece or nephew homeless."

Trill giggled. "Nieces."

His eyes widened. "What? She's having twins?"

Trill grinned. "Yep. And they have good spirits, which was my main concern."

"That's a relief." His expression became serious. "I have something to ask you. I did some research before you got up this morning. I found that in Massachusetts, a man can take the woman's last name when they marry. I'd like to take the name Song, instead of having you take Richards."

Her eyes rounded, and for several seconds, she couldn't breathe. "You'd do that for me?"

She hadn't thought out totally what marrying Adam would entail. Of course, a lot of women kept their own last names when they married, but it would mean she'd still be married to a Richards. Lucas' last name would be Song, and not the last name of the man who wanted to kill him.

Tears filled her eyes making Adam's features waver. "Have I told you in the last hour that I love you?" She threw her arms around his neck. "That is almost the best gift ever."

He chuckled. "What's the best gift?"

She kissed him. "You. You are the best gift."

***

Adam fidgeted at the table, uncomfortable in the cold gray room. He never expected to see the inside of a prison, and certainly never planned on visiting his father again. The door on the other side of the Plexiglas opened and his father followed a guard into the room. Adam hadn't seen him in nine months. His father's hair was now a dull gray, and his cheeks were hollowed. He'd always been a vibrant man, exuding power, now he seemed…broken.

Connor sat in the chair on the other side of the glass and picked up the phone.

Adam picked the one up on his side. "Hi, Dad."

"Adam, I never expected you'd come visit me."

"Me either, but, um, I thought I should be the one to tell you."

His father hunched forward.

Adam's voice cracked. "Art's dead." That was harder to say than he'd expected it to be. His brother had come so close to killing Trill, he hadn't thought he had any love left for him.

Adam explained about Trill and how Art had chased them. And how Art died, but not who shot him.

If his father had been free, he could have found a way to access police records to find out the details. His father had few questions.

Connor rubbed his face. "He was never controlled enough and always too impatient."

Adam couldn't judge his father's feelings at the news. Did it only bother him to the extent that his son was a disappointment?

Now that he'd gotten the necessary part out of the way, Adam had to ask what he needed to know. "Had you planned to sacrifice Jamie like that?"

Connor half left his chair and dropped back into it. "No! I wanted to gain power through your baby, but there was no need to kill the child or mother. She would have had to cut herself and anoint the baby with her blood. That's all. I wanted you and Jamie to be happy. That's why I encouraged you to love her. I would never have taken her away from you."

A small pain unfurled in his heart and melted away. Yes, his father was a killer, and deserved to be in prison, but now Adam knew for sure that his father loved him. "It wasn't meant to be for Jamie and me. Love can't be forced. She's happy with her husband, and I'm happy with Trill." Adam tightened his grip on the phone. "Did you love Mom?"

Connor's voice was barely a whisper. "More than anything. She was the light in my darkness. She never knew what I did to gain power. You're so much like her."

Adam stared into his father's eyes. He'd been close to his mother and there'd always been a gulf between him and his father that he'd never been able to cross. They still didn't connect, but he understood his father a little better.

"Trill and I got married last week. We're going to raise the baby together, and I hope we have more children."

His father smiled. It was the first time Adam had seen peace on his face rather than the thirst for power. "Can you send pictures?"

"Um, ah, sure." He'd never had this type of conversation with his dad before. "There's more. As backup, Art got another girl pregnant when Trill disappeared. Do you remember Pam Rochelle?"

Connor nodded. "She was a good friend of your mother's."

"It's her daughter, Bryanna. I'm helping her inherit Art's estate. She's having twin girls in October." Half-sisters to Lucas, but they would be raised as cousins.

"Thank you for telling me."

The door behind him opened and Adam glanced back. A guard stood at the door. "Dad, I have to go."

"Thanks for coming, son. I love you."

"I love you, too, Dad." He hung the phone back on the

wall. He'd probably never come back again, but he would send pictures as he promised.

THE END

The next book in the **Rawlins** series is **Kristy's Puzzle**.

A passion for cryptograms shouldn't lead to kidnapping…

Kristy Collins' visit to her best friend becomes a fight for her freedom, and maybe even her life, after she partially solves an encrypted magic spell. She needs help to stay out of the hands of power-hungry men, but unfortunately, her protector is the man whose heart she broke eighteen months ago.

Mark Simmons would rather search for terrorists in a jungle than be stuck alone with his ex-girlfriend. But after she's almost kidnapped, he reluctantly agrees to play her bodyguard. Now, he must work with Kristy to find and stop the men who want her to decrypt a spell that could give them control of anyone in their way.

Mark tries to keep his distance from Kristy, but he sees she's changed. It might be more difficult than he anticipated to preserve the walls around his heart as he protects her.

Books by Deborah Wallace

Rawlins Series
Kathleen's Legacy
Jason's Forbidden Woman
Jamie's Trials
Adam's Redemption
Kristy's Puzzle
Tony's to Protect
Abby's Salem Legacy– *Fall 2023*

Wounded Warrior Hearts Series
Wounded Warrior Hearts: Steven
Wounded Warrior Hearts: Amy
Wounded Warrior Hearts: Russ

Choice Series
Second Choice
Third Choice
No Choice
Her Choice
Series complete

Unknown Series (Romantic Suspense)
Father Unknown
Killer Unknown
Series complete

Other Books (Romantic Suspense)
I Shot the Sheriff
Your Love Belongs to Me
Summer Love
Searching for Stephanie

New Memories – Receive this book free by signing up for my newsletter on my website.

Check out my website for details on these books and where to find them. You can also sign up to receive emails when I have a new book. **www.DeborahWallaceBooks.com**.

If you can take the time, I'd love if you left a review of my book on your favorite Book sites. Thank you.

About Deborah Wallace

Someone suggested I try writing, and stories started populating my brain, begging to be put on paper (or my computer screen).

I have been called a Jane-of-all-trades, from seamstress to house and furniture designer/builder to computer programmer to technical writer and bookkeeper. I even do car maintenance. I've also guided a team of 'Future Problem Solvers'.

I grew up in Michigan, but Massachusetts has been my home for more years than I care to think about. I love the history here, the museums and antique houses, the seacoast and hiking trails.

My three children have grown and scattered, but my husband is by my side, encouraging my writing.

www.ingramcontent.com/pod-product-compliance
Lightning Source LLC
Chambersburg PA
CBHW020129180626
46810CB00004B/1467

* 9 7 8 1 9 5 1 4 5 7 0 4 4 *